Other works by Mary Lou Hagen:

Tarnished Honor
Texas Widow
Gambler's Widow

Tarnished Honor is a fast moving story set in post Civil War Texas. The main character, Matt Culhane, a bedraggled Confederate soldier, returns home to find his former life in shambles. Despite obvious problems, Matt rises above the hate and bitterness that bind so many ex-Confederate soldiers, and works toward bettering his life and the lives of those around him—regardless of any racial or political differences. Matt Culhane is brave, honest, thoughtful and a fair man—the embodiment of a true America hero. John Lory, author of *Bittersweet.*

Tarnished Honor is an excellent historical novel. It opens a new door into anti-bellum history of the Civil War. The research is solid. Best of all, the story rolls clear and solid with characters who are routinely believable. This novel deserves more attention that it is getting. Sometimes books don't delivery as promised but this one hit a home run. Mary Dresser, author of *Stand Fast, Freedom's Cost* and *The New Kingdom.*

Tarnished Honor is a historical novel that is exciting, carefully researched, and hard to put down. The characters are alive and vital and the situations they encounter are real. This book investigates a part of Texas history usually ignored—the long haul after the Civil War. Author Hagen should write us a few more exciting books about those early days. As an author of historical novels, I am impressed with her work. Mary T., Florida, U.S.A.

Texas Widow, a wonderful read, is an accurate portrayal of the Old West with just enough romance to keep this reader interested. The characters are real people, with real problems that they struggle to solve in an often hostile, unforgiving environment. But author Mary Lou Hagen also provides the reader with the details of the intimate, everyday life in the Old West. Lots of action keeps the reader engrossed in the well-told tale. Elysa Hendricks, Romance Author, Illinois, U.S.A.

Texas Widow is a fast-paced love story. I enjoyed reading this historical novel based on details of one family's true history that were passed down through several generations. It is a warm and engaging love story with many surprises and turn arounds. It held my attention all the way through. Sometimes I felt that I was seeing a Western movie in my mind's eye. I recommend it. Frances Morey, Author, Austin, Texas, U.S.A.

Texas Widow is an old fashioned love story. A rough western with a romance, it is a sweet story about two lonely people looking for fulfillment and companionship in the midst of hard times in post Civil War Texas. There is the widow, raising her children and caring for the land left to her by her late husband, and the Ranger, a courageous, mysterious man who came looking for an outlaw, not a wife. Both people are drawn together by circumstance and need. The fact the story is based on real events and real people is intriguing. Rita Gerlach, Author, Maryland, U.S.A.

In her book Gambler's Widow, Mary Lou Hagen has crafted a compelling story of the Old West. When widow Maggie DuPree travels to West Texas to help her hailing sister she encounters a world of excitement, danger and an unexpected romance with a dashing cavalry captain, Chance Richards. Through the eyes of European immigrants eager to create a new life for themselves and the Indians desperate to hold onto their way of life the reader is swept back to a time when his country was both old and new. Ms. Hagen presents the defeats and the victories, the heartbreak and the joys, as well as the challenges and the rewards of life on the Western frontier in a realistic yet personal way. I highly recommend it. Elysa Hendricks, Author, Shadow Moon.

A TASTE OF TEXAS

by

Mary Lou Hagen

Sept. 30, 2009
To Cathy & Harold, I hope
you enjoy the read.
All the best,
Mary Lou
Hagen

PublishAmerica
Baltimore

ISBN: 1-4241-5323-9
PUBLISHED BY PUBLISHAMERICA, LLLP
www.publishamerica.com
Baltimore

Printed in the United States of America

DEDICATION

To Christine Pazak, my dear friend, with love. You are the daughter I never had. May our friendship continue throughout the years to come.

ACKNOWLEDGEMENTS

As is the case with all my work, several people have helped me in various ways. First of all, I would like to thank my husband, Elvis, for all the extra duties he performed while I was struggling with this novel. His patience and understanding are priceless. I am indebted to Rosemary Croom for her review and critique of the manuscript. Her knowledge of good writing, especially plot and pace, is invaluable. To Charlene Nelson, her willingness to read my work and offer feedback is greatly appreciated. Last but certainly not least, to Francies Jagge whose knowledge of the computer far exceeds mine, you are proof that good neighbors are truly a gift.

AUTHOR'S NOTES

Having published three historical novels, I decided to turn my hand to contemporary work. A *Taste of Texas* proved to be a challenge despite the need for the endless research required by historical fiction. I admit the title is misleading in that it sounds like a cookbook. To justify, and perhaps atone for the misnomer, the reader will find authentic Texas recipes at the end of several chapters.

CHAPTER ONE

"Fire! Fire!"

The loud cry split the morning silence, and the acrid odor of burnt food hung in the air. Lyn crossed the parking lot at a run as a man in a tall white chef's hat tried to calm a group of excited people.

"Don't panic! The fire is out, but you need to stay outside for a few minutes until we're sure everything is under control."

"Paul!" Lyn's heart was pounding as she reached the people milling around. Catching her breath, she gasped, "What happened? Is anyone hurt?"

"No."

"Thank God!"

"It was only a small grease fire," Paul continued. "Lucille forgot to turn the grill off, and the degreaser ignited when she went to clean it."

"All clear," announced a muffled voice from the open doorway. A man in dark coveralls with a bandanna tied over the lower half of his face was holding a fire extinguisher in his hands.

Traces of greasy black smoke hung in the air as Lyn surveyed the kitchen. No appreciable damage had occurred. Paul and the maintenance department had acted swiftly to contain the fire, and it had not been necessary to evacuate the residents.

Lyn surveyed the smoky kitchen. "We'll have to put our emergency plans into action to cover lunch and possibly dinner. Maintenance will need some time to wash down the walls and clean the floor." Turning to the man standing beside her, she asked, "Howard, can you get started right away?"

"Sure thing, Lyn," he replied as he returned the fire extinguisher to its holder. "I'll pull a couple of guys off the mowing crew. We should have it finished by this afternoon."

Lyn took a deep breath. "Thanks, Howard."

She found Paul in the storeroom. "We need to set up temporary work stations in the employee conference room. Do the best you can with a cold menu. We can still serve in the dining room."

"Lyn, wait," Paul called as she started toward her office. "I almost forgot. Mr. MacKenzie was looking for you before the fire. When I told him you wouldn't be in till later, he got pretty upset."

Lyn smiled at Paul's sympathetic look. "That's all right, Paul. I need to talk with Dean about the temporary arrangements before I see Mr. MacKenzie."

"He's becoming a real pain," Paul said as he returned to the kitchen.

Lyn raised her head and sniffed the air. The smell of smoke still lingered, and she hoped it had not permeated the upper floors. As she turned the corner into the main hallway, she failed to see a tall form approaching from the other direction. A barrier appeared in front of her, and she walked right into it. The impact was not strong enough to knock her down, but she swayed for a moment before a pair of long arms reached out to steady her.

The man recovered first. "Are you all right? I thought you saw me or I would have called out."

Lyn took a deep breath. She was pressed tight against the firm muscles of his chest. A tremor ran down her spine, and her face colored from embarrassment. As she regained her balance, the man loosened his embrace. He dropped his arms and stepped back.

"Are you all right?" he asked again, his eyes assessing her.

"Yesss... I think so. And it was my fault for not paying attention to where I was going." Lyn's heartbeat slowed to normal.

"I confess to not being sure of where I'm going," the man laughed. "I'm looking for the accounting department."

"It's in the other wing."

"Thanks."

Lyn swallowed and her voice was scratchy when she answered. "Thank you for being so... so..." She felt like an idiot but it was the best she could do.

"I wish all my accidents were as pleasurable." His white teeth flashed in a big grin.

Blushing, she managed a weak smile, stepped around him and continued walking down the hall.

"I'm thankful we didn't have to evacuate the building," Dean Standsbury said as they discussed the fire. The administrator of The Hill Country Manor was an overweight middle-aged man of medium height.

"Yes, that would have been a traumatic experience for the residents," Lyn agreed.

"I've had some calls, but most of them are probably unaware of what happened."

"We'll try our best to play it down when they come to lunch. We're going to have an indoor picnic. That should create a relaxed atmosphere."

Thinking she needed to brief the hostess and waitresses, Lyn's gaze strayed to the windows. Her thoughts quickly turned elsewhere as she looked outside. The administrator's corner office overlooked the spacious grounds with their well-tended flowerbeds, tinkling fountains and carefully-pruned shrubbery. The picturesque view presented a picture of serenity, but its beauty eluded her now. She dreaded the meeting with MacKenzie.

Standsbury's voice brought Lyn back to the present. "We can't deny it, of course, but we don't want to publicize it, either."

Lyn nodded. "Is there anything else we need to discuss?"

"I don't think so. And Lyn, please tell Mansfield he did a good job handling what could have easily become a tragedy. I intend to speak to him personally, but I know he's very busy right now."

"I'll tell him, but I know he will appreciate hearing it from you."

Lyn hurried back to her office. It was roomy and boasted windows looking out on the patio. Soft shades of cream, slate blue and rose were coordinated with the dining room décor. A traditional cherry wood desk was flanked by two comfortable wing chairs. The matching cherry wood credenza, well-filled bookcase and two straight chairs completed the furnishings. Polished brass planters filled with greenery and an arrangement of silk flowers in a crystal vase were artfully displayed. The only personal touches Lyn permitted were a small photograph of her daughter, Samantha, on her desk, and the framed credentials of her profession on the walls.

"Ms. DeVinney! I left a message two hours ago for you to call me. Surely you can find the time someplace in your busy schedule to see to the needs of the residents."

Lyn looked up to see the scowling face of Lawrence MacKenzie. His slender frame towered over her, and she fought the urge to slide out of her chair and disappear under her desk. Instead, she smiled and rose from her chair.

"I was just going to call you, Mr. MacKenzie."

"Humph! Ms. DeVinney, you have to do something about the deplorable service in the dining room. You know I take my insulin before I come down to breakfast, and you also know I cannot wait any longer than thirty minutes to eat. My meal was fifteen minutes late, and the food was cold." His manner was frostier than the food to which he referred.

"I spoke with Mr. Standsbury, and he assured me the problem will be corrected. If conditions don't improve, I will be forced to see my attorney about canceling my lease. I can't afford to take chances with my health." Without giving her an opportunity to reply, he turned and stomped out of the room.

Off to a bad start, the day went continually downhill. The computer printouts with the new resident figures had not been updated, and she had to revise next week's menu. Most of the residents enjoyed the impromptu picnic, but she had to assure several people they had been in no danger from the fire. As the day wound to a close, Lyn was glad to leave the entire operation in the hands of the evening supervisor.

She was retrieving her purse from her desk drawer when the phone rang. As tempting as it was to let it go unanswered, she knew she wouldn't. "Dining Services, Lyn DeVinney."

"Lyn, this is Dean. Do you have a few minutes to come to my office?"

Lyn heaved a silent sigh but her voice was pleasant as she answered, "Of course."

As she entered the room, Lyn could see the back of a man's head and shoulders above the chair facing Standsbury's desk. Dean came from behind his desk, and the man seated in the chair rose and turned to face her.

Lyn stopped abruptly, her eyes wide with recognition. The man from the accident in the hallway stood before her. At the same time, she saw the look of surprise on his face and knew he was remembering their brief encounter.

"Lyn, I'd like you to meet Shelburne MacKenzie, Lawrence MacKenzie's son. Lyn DeVinney, our director of dining services," Standsbury said.

"I believe we've already met." She smiled and held out her hand, trying to ignore the rapid beating of her heart as her pulse speeded up.

Returning her handshake, he greeted her. "I'm afraid I ran Ms. DeVinney down in the hallway this morning." He grinned, explaining to Standsbury how they met. The smile vanished and he continued, "This is somewhat awkward, but I'm sure you're aware that my father is not happy at Hill Country Manor. He seems to be particularly dissatisfied with the dining services. I thought I should look into it."

Standsbury hastened to intercede. "Why don't we sit down? I'm sure this can be worked out to everyone's satisfaction."

Lyn watched from the corner of her eye as the man folded his tall form into a sitting position. His features were too rugged to be considered classically handsome. Cut short, there was a hint of red in his light brown hair. A strong jaw line and an equally strong chin gave him an air of determination, that Lyn suspected was a definite part of his personality. Gracefully arched brows, a shade darker than his hair, and thick dark lashes framed silver gray eyes.

"I'm sorry your father isn't happy at the Manor, Mr. MacKenzie. I assure you we will do everything we can to make him comfortable. I've double-checked his doctor's diet orders, and there is no problem there. Our menus are planned around low-fat, low-cholesterol recipes with modified diets in mind, and there are always fresh fruits and vegetables and diabetic desserts." She settled back in her chair.

Before MacKenzie could respond, Standsbury interjected, "Lyn is a registered dietitian, Mr. MacKenzie. Although most facilities use consultants, it is our belief that the nutritional requirements of our residents are of the utmost importance. In order to maintain our high standards, the director must be an R.D. As a matter of fact, Lyn has a master's degree in clinical nutrition. I assure you, she is fully qualified."

Lyn watched MacKenzie's reaction. The hint of a smile hovered around his mouth. She knew Standsbury's remarks smacked of an advertising brochure. After all, she had written the thing herself.

"I'm not questioning Ms. DeVinney's qualifications, Mr. Standsbury."

The brief touch of humor faded and Lyn thought she heard a soft sigh. "I will admit Dad can be difficult at times. Since my mother died last year, he hasn't been himself. I was hoping he would fit in here and make a new life for himself." The brief touch of humor had been replaced by obvious concern.

"It's unfortunate your friends, the Schumanns, were called away so soon after your father arrived," Standsbury remarked. "They might have been able to help him adjust."

"Yes, Joe and Myra were our neighbors for many years before they moved back to Texas. Their grandson is recovering from the accident, but they plan to stay in El Paso a little longer."

Turning to Lyn, he continued, "Ms. DeVinney, I know it's late, and you probably want to get home to your family. Perhaps we can meet again in a few days and discuss this further. I'm going to be in San Antonio for several months. My company, Williams Bohrn, is building the new towers at the medical center."

Lyn's eyes widened and she stared at Shelburne MacKenzie. Oh, no! Now she would have two MacKenzies to deal with.

Lyn arrived home to find Sam watching cartoons on TV. The girl jumped up and asked for permission to spend the night at a friend's house.

"You know the rules, Sam."

"But, Mom," Sam wailed, "I'm doing better now. I made eighty on the last test."

"I know, but remember our agreement." Lyn kicked off her shoes and shrugged out of her jacket. "You have to get a 'B' on your next report card before you can stay overnight at Cathy's."

Sam's mouth puckered, and Lyn's resolve wavered. It was becoming more difficult to enforce the discipline Sam needed. A single parent had to wear many hats, and sometimes the weight of those hats seemed unbearably heavy.

"But, Mom..." Sam coaxed.

Lyn swallowed her guilt and took a deep breath. Long ago she had accepted that Sam's father would never share the responsibility. Kevin had not offered marriage and had abandoned her when she refused to have an abortion. She had chosen to keep the baby and had made a life for herself and her daughter. When she had doubts about her ability to be both mother and father, she had only to look at Sam. She was a healthy, happy ten-year old although she could sway Lyn's decisions more than was good for her.

"No, Sam." Lyn's voice held a note of finality.

Sam's pert features settled into a pout. Lyn tried hard to ignore Sam's resemblance to Kevin, but her daughter shared his brown eyes and dark hair, a marked contrast with Lyn's deep blue eyes and honey-blonde locks. She forced her wayward thoughts back to the task at hand.

"You get started on your homework while I fix dinner. Maybe Cathy can go to the movies with us tomorrow afternoon."

Carrying her shoes and jacket, Lyn started down the hall.

"You're still planning to go to the Disney shows?"

"Of course, I promised, didn't I?" Lyn answered over her shoulder.

A grin replaced the frown on Sam's face. "Can I call Cathy and find out? I know she wants to go."

"Yes, but wait until after dinner. You know it's rude to call at mealtime," Lyn admonished as she disappeared into her bedroom.

"Okay." Sam headed off to tackle her homework.

Lyn opened the refrigerator and stared at her options. There was leftover pot roast and vegetables. She could add a salad and fresh fruit. Although Lyn enjoyed cooking, the task often became a busman's holiday after a trying day at The Manor. Thank God for Paul. He was responsible for food production as well as purchasing and inventory control. Her duties were administrative and clinical.

Thinking about Paul and food preparation brought to mind Shelburne MacKenzie and his father. Another meeting with the younger MacKenzie was inevitable, and Lyn had mixed emotions about seeing him again. He seemed reasonable, but where family was concerned, protective instincts always won out.

The buzzing of the microwave interrupted Lyn's introspection. She had gone through the motions of heating the leftovers, tossing a salad and setting the table while mulling over the dilemma with the MacKenzies. Shaking her head that she brought her work home too often, she placed the food on the table and called Sam to dinner.

Late the next afternoon, Lyn turned into a tree-lined street and stopped in front of a low rambling ranch house.

"Thanks, Ms. DeVinney. I had a lot of fun," Cathy called over her shoulder as she slammed the car door.

"You're welcome, Cathy."

Sam crawled into the front seat and sprawled beside her mother.

"Buckle your seat belt, Sam." Lyn glanced at her daughter. Sam's jean-clad legs straightened, and she pulled herself to an upright position. A brief flare of sadness penetrated Lyn's happy mood. Sam was growing up.

"That was fun, Mom. Thanks for taking us."

"I had fun, too. I guess I haven't outgrown the Disney films. I've always liked them."

"Don't forget, I have practice Wednesday after school. Cathy's mom is going to take us to the ball park, but she wants you to bring us home."

"I won't forget. I've already spoken with Janet."

Sam and Cathy played softball and spring practice was under way. Lyn made every effort to participate in Sam's activities, and she and Sam took part in church functions.

Lyn was happy with her life. She enjoyed her job at The Manor. One night a month she drove to San Antonio to attend the dietetic association meetings. Occasionally, she had dinner with fellow members. Since her relationship with Kevin, Lyn had shunned all opportunities to form any kind of male attachment. She smiled thinking of Bob, her sister Rhonda's husband, telling her that a fellow wouldn't need a cold shower to cool him off, that her voice and manner would freeze him to death.

They reached the apartment complex and Lyn pulled into the carport. Sam was out of the vehicle before Lyn could turn off the ignition.

"Are you gonna fix dinner?"

"Sam! You can't be hungry." Lyn locked the car doors.

"Well...I will be later."

"I'll fix a snack before we go to bed," Lyn promised.

As she drove the short distance to The Manor, Lyn was grateful the facility was located in the small town of Mt. Laurel. Reflecting on the beauty of the countryside, she was convinced there was no more beautiful sight than Texas in the spring. The budding bluebonnets and scarlet Indian paintbrush would soon cover the area with blankets of color.

Situated on a ten-acre site, The Manor's pink brick buildings contrasted with the green of the manicured lawn and the graceful, old, live oak trees that had been carefully preserved when the facility was constructed. Designed to resemble an English country estate, the three-story complex projected an air of dignity and quiet elegance. A curving driveway split several yards in front of the entrance with one section leading to a large parking lot at the side of the main building, and the other winding around to the back. Lyn pulled into her designated parking space at the back of the building.

The early morning silence was broken the minute Lyn walked into the kitchen. The clatter of dishes and cooking utensils, the hum of the equipment and raised voices, testified that this was a place of intense activity. Tantalizing odors of roasting meat and savory vegetables mingled with the yeasty aroma of baking bread.

"Good morning." Lyn raised her voice to be heard above the din. A chorus of greetings echoed back. Stopping at the baking area, she sniffed the spice-laden air.

"That cake batter smells heavenly, Patty." Lyn gestured toward the large bowl on the counter.

"It's the new recipe you wanted me to try. Do you want me to bring you a sample when it's done?" Patty grinned, a hint of mischief in her eyes.

Lyn grimaced, then sighed in defeat. "I should wait until it's tested by the staff, but …"

Patty chuckled as Lyn hurried to her office. She was shrugging into a starched white lab coat when Paul stuck his head in the door.

"Good morning, Paul."

"Good morning." He smiled, revealing even white teeth. "Do you have a minute? I'd like to go over the plans for the barbecue."

"That's a good idea," Lyn agreed, opening her desk drawer and pulling out a file folder.

"How about some coffee before we get started?"

"A man after my own heart," Lyn replied.

"I should be so lucky," he muttered under his breath as he left the room.

CHAPTER TWO

Shelburne MacKenzie closed the apartment door and pitched his keys on the coffee table. He surveyed the small living room with its southwestern color scheme in shades of beige, turquoise and melon. The place was clean, the décor fresh and the location good. As temporary quarters went, it was better than most he had found for the short periods of time he needed them. But God, he was tired of the traveling, moving from one part of the country to another, changes in climate, lifestyles, not being able to form lasting relationships and a hundred other facets of his job.

The shrill ring of the telephone cut into his thoughts. Quickly shedding his suit jacket, he pitched it on the sofa and headed for the wall phone in the kitchen. "Hello."

"Burne?" (Pronounced B-u-r-n.)

He recognized his father's voice. Just what he needed after a hard day.

"Yeah. How are you, Dad?" Knowing he was in for a lengthy conversation, Burne pulled a kitchen stool up to the phone.

"Not so good, son. I'm not sleeping very well these days, and it leaves me feeling tired most of the time."

Burne stifled a quick retort that Lawrence should find something to do during the day so he would be tired enough to sleep at night. "Have you talked with your doctor? Maybe he can give you something to help you relax."

"No, I have to make an appointment and have the van take me to his office. Ms. Chavez, she's the activities director, said the schedule was full for tomorrow."

"Will you be able to go in a few days?" Burne tugged at his tie. He managed to loosen it and unfasten the top button on his shirt.

"I don't know. When are you coming to see me, son? I thought when you were sent to San Antonio you would be spending some time with me. I've only seen you once since you got here," Lawrence said, his voice filled with self-pity.

"I'm sorry, Dad. I've been pretty busy getting the apartment set up, leasing a vehicle and a dozen other things. I spent the entire afternoon at the steel workers union trying to work out a reciprocity agreement. Those guys can argue more and say less than any bunch I know," Burne chuckled. "But I know where they're coming from. I felt the same way when I was working with them while I was in school."

He thought for a moment. "Tell you what. I'll take you out to dinner tomorrow night. How's that?"

"I'd like that, but why don't we eat in the dining room here? That will give you a chance to see for yourself what I've been telling you about this place."

Burne needed to send reports to the home office, but they could wait. He knew his father was lonely.

"That's fine with me, Dad. What time should I be there?"

"The dining room opens at four thirty and they quit serving at six thirty. I know that's early for you, but most of the residents don't like to eat late."

"No problem. I'll knock off early, and we'll have time to visit before dinner. Anne sent you the latest pictures of the kids, and I unpacked them last night."

"I miss the children a lot more than I thought I would. It seemed like it was so noisy and everything was always in a turmoil when I was there, but now …"

Burne heard the sadness in his father's voice and a feeling of helplessness and frustration washed over him. Lawrence did not seem interested in anything. Well, he had six months to try to help his father. That was the major reason he had volunteered for the San Antonio assignment.

"I haven't eaten yet, Dad, and I need to do some more unpacking. I'll see you tomorrow around five."

"All right, son. Good night."

"Good night, Dad." Burne hung up the phone, his mood altered even more after the conversation with his father. Removing his tie, he unfastened the next three buttons of his shirt. A cold beer was just what he needed, and he took a can from the refrigerator. Feet propped on the coffee table, Burne took a drink of the icy liquid and let it trickle down his throat. He settled back in the chair and let his mind wander. A sardonic grin played around his lips as the thought about how he had wanted to travel when he got out of school.

Before the ink was dry on his college diploma, Burne enlisted in the Air Force. Afterward, he was ready to stay in one place for a while. His experience in construction coupled with his degree in business administration landed him the job with Williams Bohrn.

Three years later when one of the representatives retired, he moved into the field. The work was interesting; he moved from job to job and was caught up in problems ranging from expediting material to union negotiations. He was thirty-five years old. How much longer did he want to continue his present way of life?

* * *

Muted sounds from the dining room, and the faint aroma of good food penetrated Lyn's concentration as she studied a new resident's file. It was dinnertime and her busy day was almost over. Placing the file in her desk drawer, she left her office to check with the hostess before leaving.

"Everything okay, Becky?"

"Everything's fine," Becky answered, her smile revealing the dimple in her cheek. With a discrete motion of her head, she whispered, "Is he for real?"

Lyn glanced at the diners. "Is who for real?"

"The hunk with Mr. MacKenzie?"

Lyn felt her stomach lurch and knew without a doubt that Becky was referring to Shelburne MacKenzie. Slowly turning her head, her fears were confirmed. The man was indeed dining with his father. At least his back was turned.

"That's Mr. MacKenzie's son. His company sent him here on the tower project at the medical center." Lyn's voice was steady, betraying none of the trepidation she was feeling.

"That means he'll be around for awhile."

Becky's pleased smile was not lost on Lyn. Good heavens! Although she hadn't noticed a wedding ring, that didn't mean the man wasn't married. At his age and with his looks, he probably was. Lyn made it a firm rule to stay out of her employee's personal lives. Unless it caused a problem with her job, it was none of her business if Becky wanted to get involved with Shelburne MacKenzie, but still...

"Isn't he a little old for you?" Lyn forced a teasing note into her voice.

"I like mature men," Beck quipped as she turned to the couple waiting to be seated.

The waitresses were college students, and their youthful enthusiasm was like a breath of fresh air to the residents. Uniforms reminiscent of colonial times with calf-length skirts and frilly mop caps lent a touch of authenticity to the décor.

"Lyn, Lyn, over here." A woman rose from her chair and beckoned to her. Lyn threaded her way between the tables, most of them occupied. She was grateful she did not have to pass the MacKenzies but knew she couldn't leave the dining room without speaking to them.

"I just received some new pictures of my grandson. I want to show them to you." The proud grandmother held out an envelope stuffed to overflowing.

Lyn scanned the pictures, trying to come up with an original remark or two. The toddler was a handsome little boy, obviously the apple of this grandmother's eye.

"He is adorable, Mrs. Houseman. And he certainly has grown since they visited last summer. How old is he now?"

"Jeremy is twenty-seven months old. I think he looks just like my son but, of course, his mother says he favors her side of the family." The woman's laugh said she didn't really care who her grandson looked like. She was happy to be his grandmother.

Returning the pictures, Lyn spoke to several of the residents as she made her way toward the door. She took a deep breath and braced herself for Lawrence MacKenzie's negative remarks as she walked toward the table. Shelburne MacKenzie was on his feet in an instant.

"Please, Mr. MacKenzie, sit down and finish your dinner. I just wanted to say hello and inquire if everything is satisfactory." She turned a bright smile in their direction.

Before Burne could reply, his father spoke up. "Ms. DeVinney, you'll forgive me if I don't get up. My arthritis is bothering me." With a slight wave toward Burne, he added, "I understand you've met my son."

Lyn glanced at the younger MacKenzie. He had remained standing. "Yes, we've met. Please sit down. Your food is getting cold." With a weak smile she continued, "Hot food hot, cold food cold." At his puzzled expression her smile broadened, and she explained, "First rule of good food service management."

"Humph!"

Lyn heard Lawrence's grunt but chose to ignore it. Burne returned her smile, sat down and picked up his fork. "We need to get together, Ms. DeVinney."

"Of course. Please call me, and we'll set up an appointment."

"Thanks, I'll do that." He smiled.

"Enjoy your dinner." She could feel Shelburne's eyes following her as she walked away. Slender, but subtly curved in all the right places, her navy skirt and pale blue blouse fit her to perfection. Shapely legs clad in dark hose, she stood approximately five feet six inches tall in her low-heeled shoes.

"Good night, Lyn. Give Sam a big hug for me."

"I'll do that. Good night, Becky."

Lyn left The Manor with a sigh of relief. Why did Lawrence MacKenzie and his son make her uncomfortable? She had dealt with difficult residents and their families before. She replayed the conversation searching for clues. Had Shelburne MacKenzie seemed a little friendlier? Were his gray eyes a trifle warmer, his smile a bit more sincere?

Her mind's eye could see the pale blue shirt, the paisley tie, and navy blazer. With a start, she realized her mind was drifting in a direction she had no intention of allowing it to go. Years of determined practice enabled her to force her thoughts to the evening ahead. Sam would be hungry and there was laundry to be done.

* * *

Bright spring sunshine flooded the ball diamond where fifteen girls, ranging from ages eight through twelve, clustered around a shapely young woman with a long blonde braid hanging down her back. Two sets of weathered wooden bleachers faced each other across the playing area, which was bordered by neatly mowed grass and huge live oak trees.

"I'd kill for hair like that," Janet Thompson confessed to Lyn as they watched their daughters during the first practice session of the season.

"If you'd quit cutting it every other week, it just might grow out," Lyn teased.

"I could let it grow forever, but it would never look like that." Janet wore her dark hair in a pixie cut which suited her petite features. In denim cut-offs and an oversize tee shirt, she looked almost young enough to be one of the players.

Lyn felt like a giant when they were together, but they were good friends. Lyn favored slacks over shorts, and her khaki twills were topped with a pink cotton blouse.

"How are things going at The Manor?" Janet inquired.

"I'm not sure. Mr. MacKenzie seems a little more satisfied, but it's hard to tell. His son wants to talk with me so I guess there are still some problems."

"His son?"

"Yes. His name is Shelburne, and he's going to be in San Antonio for several months."

"Shelburne?" Janet cocked an eyebrow.

"Don't let his name fool you. There's nothing wimpy about the man." Lyn deliberately kept her eyes focused on the activity on the field.

"Oh? What's he like?"

A mental image of Shelburne MacKenzie flashed through Lyn's mind. She chewed her lip for a moment. "Well, I'd say he's about thirty-five, tall, very well turned out—clothes, neat hair style, you know." She noticed the coach had gathered the girls together for a pre-practice conference.

"Uhm. Is he married?" Janet turned to watch the players as they gathered around the coach.

Her nonchalant behavior did not fool Lyn. "I don't know. He doesn't wear a wedding ring, but that doesn't mean anything. I would be inclined to think he is, but he probably doesn't let that stop him."

"My, don't you sound cynical. Not all men are heels, you know. After all, look at Charley."

"I keep telling you how lucky you are. Charley is one of a kind. Anyway, I just hope Shelburne MacKenzie doesn't cause me any more problems. I have enough already."

The tightly knit group below erupted and girls ran in all directions.

"Batter up," yelled the young woman with the long braid. Practice was underway.

"We need to stop at Bargains Galore," Lyn told Sam as they left the ballpark.

"Yeah!" Sam's face was flushed, and one side was streaked with dirt.

"As soon as we get there, go wash your face and hands," Lyn instructed.

"Can we stop at the snack bar? I'm hungry," Sam complained.

"If you promise to eat a salad with your burger and fries."

Sam grimaced. "Okay."

Lyn wheeled her cart down the aisle. Toothpaste, mouthwash, Tylenol, she mentally surveyed the contents of the medicine cabinet.

"Ms. DeVinney?" A rich masculine voice sounded close by.

Startled, she looked up and found herself face to face with Shelburne MacKenzie. Her eyes went wide and she gaped.

He grinned, revealing even white teeth.

"Mr. MacKenzie," her voice ended on a high note.

"Since we're going to be seeing each other for the next few months, do you think you could call me Burne?"

"Burne?" Lyn parroted.

"Short for Shelburne. It was my mother's maiden name, but Dad said it was too much of a mouthful. He shortened it to Burne."

As he spoke, Lyn covertly appraised his tall frame clad in faded jeans, a yellow knit shirt and scuffed running shoes. His hair appeared more red than brown in the bright light. He looked a lot different than he did in his perfectly tailored business attire.

"My name is really Lynette, but everyone calls me Lyn." Her hands tightened on the cart handle.

"Lynette DeVinney. Sounds French."

"It is, sort of. The DeVinneys came from Alsace Lorraine originally. But that was a long time ago." She avoided looking directly at him.

"Mom, let's eat! I'm starving." Sam, her face clean, her jeans dusty, stopped in front of them. Her dark hair was pulled back in a ponytail.

Lyn gave her daughter a stern look. "Don't be rude, Sam. Mr. Mac…Burne, my daughter, Samantha. This is Mr. MacKenzie, Sam. His father is a resident at The Manor."

Before Burne could acknowledge the introduction, Sam blurted out, "The old man who gripes all the time?"

Lyn's face flushed a bright red, and she closed her eyes for a brief moment. She couldn't look at Burne, but turned to Sam, her voice stern and demanded, "Sam! Apologize this instant."

Burn's laughter erupted. Lyn realized he was not offended, but that didn't lessen her embarrassment.

"So, this is Sam." Amusement underlined his words.

Sam had the good grace to blush, and she swallowed hard trying to find her voice. "I …I'm sorry, Mr. MacKenzie."

"Apology accepted. I'll be the first to admit that Dad can be difficult, but…" his voice trailed off.

"I understand," Lyn sympathized. "The adjustment has to have been difficult. It just takes time, more for some than others."

"I suppose you're right," Burne sighed.

Lyn saw the flash of pain that darkened his gray eyes. Burne MacKenzie was evidently a man whose feelings ran deep.

"Please call me as soon as it's convenient. I'm sure there's something we can do to help your father."

"I will and thanks."

The silence grew awkward.

"Well, it was nice seeing you…Burne. I promised Sam we'd grab a sandwich. She had ball practice this morning and, as you heard, she's starving," Lyn's voice held a hint of laughter.

"I'm on my way to see Dad. He asked me to stop and pick up a few things." Burne indicated the bag he was carrying.

"Excuse me! You're blocking the aisle."

An agitated voice sounded behind Lyn. Moving to let the woman pass, Lyn and Burne found themselves mere inches apart. Silver gray eyes stared into deep blue ones. Lyn dropped her gaze, breaking the contact. Her throat felt too dry to speak.

"Nice to see you, Lyn; and to meet you, Sam. I'm sure we'll see each other again soon. Have a nice day." Burne winked at Sam, then grinned as he walked away.

CHAPTER THREE

"It's time for the care conference. I'll be in the nursing unit if you need me," Lyn told Paul as she left the kitchen.

The Manor provided a health care facility for its residents. If they became incapacitated, the nursing unit took over. Lyn was responsible for their nutritional needs. She held a weekly meeting with Barbara Neal, Director of Nurses, and Theresa Martinez, the diet clerk who supervised mealtime and did the daily charting.

Lyn entered the nursing unit to find Theresa gathering an armload of charts. "Here, let me help you with those."

"Thanks." The young woman smiled.

Theresa was a beautiful young woman. Her dark eyes and hair and flawless olive complexion, traits of her Hispanic heritage, were emphasized by her immaculate white uniform. Lyn knew Theresa's outward beauty was a true reflection of her inner self. She treated the residents with respect and was genuinely interested in their welfare.

As they passed Barbara's office, she looked up from her desk, smiled and said, "Be right with you."

Lyn and Theresa continued on to the conference room.

"Any particular problems?" Lyn asked as Barbara joined them.

"Mrs. Grimes has lost two more pounds. I've talked with Dr. Hayden. He wants a conference with you and her husband," Barbara reported.

Lyn flipped through the charts and pulled one free. Quickly scanning the entries, she nodded. "I'll call him as soon as I get back to my office. I can add more supplement feedings, but she's not taking all we give her now."

Turning to Theresa she asked, "How did she respond to the change in formula?"

Theresa shook her head; her dark eyes filled with compassion. "I don't think she even noticed. It's hard to tell since she rarely makes a sound. You have to watch her eyes carefully."

Lyn nodded in agreement. "I know it's difficult, Theresa. Just do the best you can. But then," she smiled at the young woman, "you always do."

The remainder of the meeting went quickly, and Barbara excused herself to return to her office. Lyn checked each chart and made appropriate notations. The two women gathered up the records and returned them to the nurses' station.

As Lyn reached her desk, the phone rang. "Dining Services, Lyn DeVinney."

"Hello, Lyn. Burne MacKenzie. How are you?"

Caught off guard, Lyn's heart skipped a beat. A mental image of the man flashed across her mind.

"Hello, Mr. MacKenzie."

"Mr. MacKenzie? I thought we were on a first name basis."

"I'm sorry. I just this minute got back to my office. I've been in a meeting."

"Would you rather I call back later?"

"Oh, no. I assume you're calling about your father?" She sat down at her desk and pulled her calendar forward.

"Yes. When would be convenient for us to get together?"

"What about your schedule? I'm sure you're very busy."

"Things usually slow down in late afternoon."

Lyn scanned the calendar. "Is four o'clock tomorrow afternoon convenient for you?"

"Yes, that's fine. I plan to drive out and visit Dad. Maybe I'll stay and have dinner with him."

Lyn penciled in the time on the calendar. "I'm sure he would like that. You know, you may dine here as often as you like. Just pick up a guest ticket at the desk and give it to the hostess. The billing is done monthly and guest meals are billed separately."

"You mean Dad gets stuck with my tab?" There was a hint of laughter in his voice.

"Only if you choose not to pay it."

"Good thing I'm on an expense account."

"I can't see you taking advantage of your father," Lyn answered. She unconsciously underlined the note on her calendar.

"No. His responsibility to me ended a long time ago." With a change of subject, he continued. "I'd better let you get back to your work. I'll see you tomorrow afternoon. Goodbye, Lyn."

"Goodbye." Her mood pensive, Lyn slowly replaced the receiver.

"Mom, don't forget the game Saturday. Is my uniform ready?" Sam asked for the third time.

"Sam, I told you! It's been washed and pressed," Lyn answered, agitation plain in her tone. She put the iron down and pulled a blouse from the clothesbasket.

"Just checking, just checking."

"You'd better get busy on your homework. You still need to improve your math scores." She tested the iron and turned the temperature down.

"Ah, Mom. There's this neat show on the Family Channel I want to watch."

"You know the rules. No TV until your homework is finished."

Sam opened her mouth to protest, looked at Lyn's face and decided against it.

A light tap sounded and Lyn looked up to see Burne standing in her office doorway. She had been alternating between anticipation and dread all day.

"Hello." He grinned, his smile crinkling the creases around his eyes. It was evident he spent a lot of time outdoors.

Lyn rose and came from around her desk to welcome him. "Hello, Burne. Come in. You're right on time."

His hair was windblown. He was wearing khaki pants and a light blue shirt. A navy windbreaker was slung over his shoulder.

"Hope you don't mind the informality, but your Texas weather makes a tie da…darn uncomfortable."

Lyn smiled at his near slip of the tongue and shook her head. "You'll find people tend to dress casually here. As for the weather now, wait until it's really summer. This is only a preview."

"I'm aware of that. In fact, I spent a summer in Phoenix a few years ago. It can't get any hotter than that!"

"No, but you'll find the humidity a lot higher, so be prepared. Please, do sit down." Lyn indicated the chairs facing her desk. She moved back behind the desk. Her beige linen skirt and peach silk blouse, with the collar buttoned to her throat, gave only a hint of her feminine attributes.

"By the way, how is Sam?" There was a mischievous twinkle in his gray eyes.

"She's fine," Lyn replied. A faint blush colored her cheeks as she recalled Sam's outburst concerning his father. "She's all excited about the first game of the season on Saturday morning."

"Game?" Burne sat down across from her.

"Sam plays on a softball team sponsored by the local supermarket."

"When and where do they play?"

Lyn's eyes narrowed slightly. Why would Burne be interested in a girl's softball team?

"I thought it might be something Dad would like to watch. He used to be into Little League when my brother and I were growing up."

"You're certainly welcome to come. The ballpark is on the south edge of town on Jackson Street. Coming from San Antonio, you can't miss it. The game starts at nine o'clock."

"Thanks, maybe I can get him interested. It's worth a try." Burne relaxed and stretched his long legs out in front of him.

Lyn nodded. "This problem with your father. Tell me, what can we do to help him?" She leaned forward and clasped her hands on the desktop.

"I'm sure you know it's not his diet as much as his state of mind."

"I agree that's probably part of it, but we want to do everything we can to see that he enjoys the food and is pleased with the service. Maybe you could tell me more about his food preferences. There are hundreds of diabetic recipes and prepared foods to choose from. We'll be glad to include anything that appeals to him."

Burn's expression grew thoughtful. "That's a hard one to answer. You see, his diabetes is a recent diagnosis. It developed after my mother died so there's no history to fall back on."

"Before he became diabetic, what did he particularly enjoy?"

Burne's gaze strayed to the windows behind Lyn's desk. He stared at the white, wrought-iron patio furniture and the pots of colorful blooming flowers. His voice was husky when he answered. "My mother was an excellent cook. She did a lot of baking. Dad is a meat and potatoes man, steak, roast, et cetera. Not too keen on fruit and vegetables."

"That does make it more difficult. I'll go over the recipes and do some research. I'm sure we can come up with new dishes he will enjoy." Lyn scribbled a note on the pad in front of her.

"I really appreciate your help. If he could just come to terms with Mom's death, I think he would be all right. I know there are lots of activities here for him, but he just isn't interested."

"I'm glad to do what I can to help." Lyn pursed her lips and thought for a moment. "Have you talked with Marjorie Chavez, our activities director?"

"I've heard Dad mention her, but we haven't met."

"Talking with her might help. Margie probably isn't aware of the circumstances. Sometimes a little encouragement can do wonders."

"Sounds like a good idea. Could you set up an appointment for me?"

"Yes, of course." Lyn reached for the phone. When Margie answered, she explained the purpose of her call. "I'm not sure, Margie. I'll ask him." Looking up at Burne, she inquired, "Would you like to meet with her now?"

"Yes, if she has the time." Burne straightened in his chair.

Lyn relayed the message. Pointing toward the front of the building, she explained, "Her office is in the other wing. Take the hallway to the lobby, turn left, and it's the first door on your right." She rose but remained standing behind her desk.

Burne quickly came to his feet. "Thanks for your help. I really appreciate it. Will I see you later?"

Lyn's heartbeat quickened, but she shook her head. "I don't think so. I usually check the dining room before I leave, but I'll probably be gone when you and your father come down to dinner."

Lyn thought she saw a look of disappointment appear on Burne's face. It vanished before she could be sure.

"Tell Sam hello for me." He flashed a grin as he left the room.

* * *

Lyn felt the bleachers settle as the space next to her was occupied. She was watching the activity on the field and had failed to notice Burne and his father approaching. She smiled and acknowledged their presence. She smelled the clean scent of Burne's cologne and every nerve in her body tingled.

"Good morning."

Both men returned her greeting, and Lyn saw the older man's eyes focus on the ball game. He watched silently for several minutes, then turned to Lyn.

"Burne tells me you have a little girl on the Owls team."

"Yes, she's the first baseman. Her name is Sam."

The white uniform with brown numbers was easy to identify.

The opposing team, the Lone Star Ladies, representing a commercial laundry in San Antonio, wore red, white and blue. Eighteen young girls were scattered over the field as the players exchanged positions. The crowd yelled encouragement and advice.

Janet and Charley were seated on the other side of Lyn, and she made hurried introductions. She glanced out of the corner of her eye, saw Burne watching her and quickly forced her attention on the scene below.

The Owls were coming up to bat. The score was three to four in their favor.

The umpire called two strikes then Sam's bat connected, and she sent the ball soaring into the outfield. She took off running and, by the time she gained first base, the outfielder was searching for the ball that had gone over her head. The Owl rooters were on their feet screaming encouragement as Sam rounded the field. She made it to third base before the ball was caught by the baseman.

"That 'a girl, Sam." Janet and Charley were on their feet yelling as enthusiastically as Lyn.

Lyn grabbed Burne's arm and screamed, "Don't run, Sam!" As her fingers made contact with his forearm, Lyn's eyes went wide. She turned to see him grinning at her. Before she could take her hand away, he placed his own over it and covered hers. Lyn refused to meet his eyes, and he withdrew his hand. She let go of his arm.

The Owls rooters were screaming encouragement while the Lone Star Lady fans booed and gave out with catcalls to distract the batter. The next play brought Sam home safe, but the inning was over when the next batter struck out.

"Tough luck." Burne turned to Lyn with a sympathetic smile.

"Yes," Lyn nodded but did not look at him.

The game progressed with the opposing team racking up two runs to tie the score at five-all. Cathy came up to bat and hit a short ball to left field. Her chubby legs didn't move fast enough, and she failed to make it to first base.

The umpire called an out, Janet and Charley groaned, and a disappointed Lyn exclaimed, "Oh, no!"

Play continued and Lyn tried to keep her attention on the game, but Burne's presence was disconcerting. Their shoulders brushed from time to time, and she knew he was watching her from the corner of his eye. From furtive glances at the elder MacKenzie, she couldn't tell if he was enjoying himself.

Finally, it was all over, and the Owls were defeated seven to five. The disgruntled fans began leaving the bleachers while the victor's supporters swarmed onto the field.

"We're taking the kids to Dairy Bar," Janet remarked. Turning to the MacKenzies, she said, "You're welcome to join us."

Burne looked at his father, his expression hopeful, but Lawrence shook his head and replied, "Thank you for asking, but I'm a bit tired. Maybe another time."

"Sure," Janet answered. Charley excused himself to go down to the playing field.

Not bothering to hide his disappointment, Burne turned to Lyn. "Tell Sam I'm sorry the Owls lost."

"I'll tell her," Lyn said.

"I plan to drive out to The Manor one evening next week. Maybe I'll see you then."

There didn't seem to be any way to answer without sounding anxious so Lyn just nodded. She watched as Burne followed his father to the parking lot.

"So that's Burne MacKenzie. Quite a hunk, I'd say." Janet was openly admiring the man's backside as he descended the bleachers.

Lyn followed Janet's gaze and admitted, but only to herself, that he filled out the faded jeans quite well.

The subdued Owls swarmed into Dairy Bar. The girls drowned their disappointment in hamburgers and french fries.

"Janet, will you be taking the kids to New Braunfels for next week's game?" Mary Ann Brach asked. Her daughter, Lisa, played on the team.

"Probably," Janet confirmed, turning to Lyn. "Didn't you say you might have to work?"

"Yes, it's possible. I'm working on the summer menus plus we have a big barbecue coming up in a few weeks."

Soon afterward, the group split up, and Lyn and Sam drove off. There were errands to run.

"We're having spaghetti for dinner, Sam. Why don't you shower while I get it started?" Lyn walked into the kitchen and washed her hands at the sink.

"Mom, why did Mr. MacKenzie and his dad come to the ball game?" Sam asked as they lingered over fresh fruit and homemade sugar cookies.

Lyn knew the primary reason was to help the elder MacKenzie's state of mind, but instinct told her it was more than that. She nibbled on a cookie as she tried to formulate a sensible answer.

"I don't know except Burne told me he used to be in Little League when he was a boy."

"He did? I wonder if his team ever won any championships?"

"You'll have to ask him about that. He may come to your next home game." Lyn watched covertly for Sam's reaction.

"Well, he's not bad looking—for an old guy, that is." Sam grinned, her eyes alight with mischief.

"Old guy? Why, he's probably around my age," Lyn pretended to be indignant.

Sam burst out laughing. "Gets you every time, doesn't it, Mom?" Then her face lost its amused look. "Say, you're not...you know...?"

Lyn's cheeks felt warm, but she hoped the muted light in the dining area hid the telltale blush from Sam. "I'm not sure what you're trying to say, Sam. You and I are doing just fine without a man in our life." Her voice sounded weak in her own ears.

Sam eyed her mother, and Lyn knew her daughter was not satisfied with her answer. Burne MacKenzie was interested in more than bringing his father to watch Sam play softball.

CHAPTER FOUR

Burne leaned back in his chair and propped his feet on the desk. After several hours in the hot sun, the air-conditioned construction office felt like heaven. Andy Crawford, project engineer, and Manuel Garza, the timekeeper, had left for the day. Burne's thoughts strayed to an ice-cold beer. He closed his eyes and could almost feel the refreshing liquid slide down his throat. The door slammed and Burne brought his feet to the floor. He swiveled in his chair to face Pete Martinez, the steelworker's foreman.

"I brought the time cards in. The men have left and it's time to call it a day." He placed the cards on Manuel's desk and turned to face Burne.

"Yeah. I was thinking the same thing myself."

"You gonna visit your father tonight?"

"No, I don't think so. It's been a long day and I'm beat." Burne rose, stretched his neck and flexed his shoulders, trying to work the kinks out of his tired muscles.

Pete hesitated a moment, then asked, "You care to go for a beer? There's a little place not far from here. It's quiet and a guy can relax and enjoy a cold one."

Burne grinned. Pete must have been reading his mind. "Sounds good to me. Lead the way and I'll follow."

When they were seated in the bar with frosted mugs of beer, Pete spoke first. "Burne, I've been meaning to ask you. What's the name of the place where your father lives?"

"Hill Country Manor. It's in Mt. Laurel," Burne replied, his curiosity mildly aroused. Pete nodded. "That's what I thought. My baby sister works there. She's a diet clerk in the nursing unit. She mentioned seeing the name MacKenzie when she was using the computer. I just put two and two together."

"Does she work for Lyn DeVinney?" Burne kept his tone casual.

"Yeah. She really likes her, too. Says Ms. DeVinney treats her good and gives her credit when she does a good job. She does seem like a nice person." He took another swallow of his beer.

"You know Lyn?" Burne felt a strange twinge of jealousy. Pete was a good-looking fellow with thick black hair and sensual dark eyes.

"No, I don't really *know* her, but I've met her. The Manor has an employee-of-year banquet, and I've escorted Theresa a couple of times. She won last year," he added proudly.

"Congratulations. I guess they treat their employees well." Burne savored the bitter tang of the cold brew.

"Theresa has worked there since she got out of high school. She likes working with the old people."

"That's unusual for a young person. She sounds like an exceptional young woman."

Pete grinned, his teeth a slash of white in his dark face. "Yeah, she sure is. She's real pretty, too."

The after-work crowd began filling the bar, and the pungent smell of smoke and liquor hung in the air. It seemed to be a neighborhood watering hole. Customers exchanged greetings and several of them were gathered around a large round table in the rear of the building.

"How old is your sister?" Burne took another swallow of beer.

"Twenty-two."

"I'm surprised she isn't married." Burne wasn't particularly interested. The comment was just something to keep the conversation going.

"Oh, she dates now and then, but she's in no hurry. The family is glad, but we don't tell her that. We hope she finds a guy who deserves her. Theresa is real special."

"Sometimes the right person just doesn't come along. I know. I'm thirty-five and I haven't found her yet." An image of honey-blond hair and deep blue eyes flashed through Burne's mind.

"I'll bet you've had a good time looking." Pete grinned, a knowing look in his eyes.

"It's been interesting at times," Burne admitted as he polished off the last of his beer.

* * *

"I think that takes care of everything. Or did I miss anything?" Lyn and Paul were seated in her office going over the plans for the barbecue to be held in two weeks.

"Do you know how many reservations we have?" Paul asked.

"At this point, we have over a hundred, but we'll get more, I'm sure," Lyn answered as she glanced at the file.

The annual barbecue provided the residents an opportunity to entertain their families and friends in an informal atmosphere. The spacious grounds accommodated a large gathering and Margie planned a number of activities for young and old.

"How about the nursing unit? Are there any changes there?"

"None that I'm aware of. Theresa has things under control. As always." Lyn smiled thinking of the conscientious young woman.

"She's good at her job, no doubt about that." Paul agreed.

"Yes, she is, and I would like to see her continue her education. She's taken the required courses for diet clerk, of course, but she's capable of so much more." Lyn shook her head.

"Well, she's still young. She may decide to go on later."

"I hope so, although it would be hard to give her up."

Lyn watched Paul as the conversation gained depth. She wondered if he had ever asked Theresa out. No gossip had filtered through the grapevine. He seemed to admire Theresa, and he couldn't be immune to her beauty. She put the idea out of her mind. It was really none of her business.

As he picked up his clipboard to leave Paul spoke, his tone casual. "By the way, I hear the Owls lost their first game."

"Yes, I'm sorry to say they did. Five to seven. The Lady Lone Stars have evidently added some good players to their team. Last year the Owls beat them easily. Nine to three, I think."

"That's right. I was there, remember? I'm sorry I couldn't make it this time, but I had a dental appointment."

"That's all right. You're lucky to have a dentist that has office hours on Saturday."

"He's only in one Saturday a month. It seems easier for me to go then than try to make it on a week day."

"You can always use your personal time, Paul. That's what it's for." Lyn reminded him.

"I know," Paul nodded, "but I like to save it. You never know when you might need it. By the way, I heard Mr. MacKenzie and his son went to Sam's game."

"Yes, they did. Burne and his brother used to be in Little League when they were growing up, and he thought it might help his father's depression."

"The man does seem pretty unhappy." He stood up. "I'd better check the inventory and get busy with the ordering."

Lyn backed out of her parking space and started for home. As she reached the split in the driveway, a dark blue Suburban turned into the visitor's parking area. There was something familiar about the shape of the driver's head and shoulders. She slowed down and watched as the man climbed out of the vehicle. As he straightened to full height, Lyn recognized Burne MacKenzie. He was bare headed, and the bright sunshine turned his sandy hair to pale copper. Wearing charcoal chinos and a pale gray knit shirt, she imagined what the choice of colors did to his silver gray eyes. *This is ridiculous. Stop it!* She pushed down on the accelerator, and the car shot forward. Burne looked in her direction just as she drew even with him. Lyn pretended to concentrate on her driving, but her pulse sped up. She could feel him watching her as she turned into the street.

※ ※ ※

As he finished the last bite of cherry pie and followed it with a swallow of perfectly brewed coffee, Burne saw that his father had eaten all of his fruited Jell-O. That was a good sign. Maybe he was finally adjusting to The Manor and his new lifestyle.

"I had a letter from Joe and Myra today," the elder MacKenzie related.

"Is their grandson completely recovered?"

"He's doing fine and should be able to play basketball when the season starts."

"That's good news. Did they say when they were coming home?"

Burne placed his fork on the empty plate and gave a sigh of satisfaction. The meal had been excellent.

"Not exactly, but they want to be here for the barbecue."

"Barbecue?"

"Oh." The older man looked chagrined. "I guess I forgot to mention it. It's a week from Saturday. They have one every year. The residents invite their families and friends. There's games and music. Dancing after the meal. It's quite a shindig from what I hear. You will come, won't you?"

"Sounds good. I'm already looking forward to it."

* * *

"I wish you could come to the game, Mom," Sam complained as she carried her empty cereal bowl to the sink.

"I do too, sweetheart, but you know I have to work today. The barbecue is too important to dump all the responsibility on Paul."

"I know, but I'll miss you in the bleachers cheering for me."

"I'll be there in spirit. Now hurry and get your things together. Janet will be here any minute."

Sam collected her tote bag and was soon on her way out the door.

Lyn surveyed the contents of her closet. Barbecues called for jeans and boots, but she needed more comfortable footwear, and she never wore jeans to work-related functions. A denim skirt and print blouse would lend a casual appearance yet be durable enough to retain a semblance of freshness. Deciding on low-heeled navy sandals, she headed for the shower.

The late morning hours were a flurry of activity as the entire food service staff put the finishing touches on the mountains of food needed for the barbecue. The buffet meal would be served on the patio, and

Paul had been tending the briskets at the barbecue grills since early morning.

Lunch was a noisy affair with everybody excited about the activities to come. Many of the residents were in western attire, and colorful shirts, skirts, jeans and boots were plentiful.

Lyn was spending a few quiet minutes in her office. The new menus needed her attention, but the revelry from the barbecue made concentration difficult.

"Hard at work, I see. Don't you ever take time off?" A rich masculine voice sounded from the doorway.

Lyn didn't have to look up to know it was Burne. Raising her head, she focused her gaze on the tall form leaning against the doorframe. He was smiling, and his white teeth emphasized his tanned complexion. The hot Texas sun had darkened his skin a shade or two. His jeans lacked the faded look she had seen before, and the fit was even better. A tartan plaid shirt stretched across his broad chest, and the short sleeves revealed muscular tanned arms covered with a sprinkling of sandy hair.

Lyn forced herself to meet his eyes. "Yes, I do take time off. In fact, I rarely work weekends, but this is a special event."

"So I hear. I think even Dad is a little excited about it."

Lyn rose and came from behind her desk. "I'm glad to hear that."

"Now that Joe and Myra are back, I don't think he'll be as lonely."

"It should help." Lyn nodded in agreement.

Burne straightened up as Lyn approached and stepped out of the doorway.

"Are you interested in any of the activities? There's volley ball, horse shoes, croquet and several other things to do," Lyn suggested. She tried to ignore the giddy feeling his presence created.

"When I arrived a few minutes ago and found Dad and the Schumanns on the patio, Myra was trying to get Dad to play croquet.

But I don't think she'll have much luck."

"Perhaps he'll play later. Would you like a cold drink? There's lemonade and iced tea."

"Will you join me?"

With every intention of refusing, Lyn suddenly found herself agreeing. "I could use a break."

Burne stepped aside as she exited the room, and he followed her down the hallway.

Lyn chose iced tea while Burne opted for lemonade, and they found a couple of unoccupied chairs.

Taking a swallow of the tart liquid, Burne sighed, "That hits the spot."

Lyn was acutely aware of his presence close beside her. She sipped her iced tea and tried to relax. There was a hollow feeling in the pit of her stomach, and her breathing seemed to be restricted.

"Tell me about yourself, Lyn. Are you a native Texan?"

Lyn stiffened and her pleasant expression hardened. She hesitated a moment, then answered, her voice cool, "Yes, I was born and raised in San Antonio."

"I didn't mean to pry. It's just that native Texans seem so proud of their ancestry." Burne shifted in his chair and watched her reaction.

Lyn's smile broke through her reserve. "Oh, we are! There's nothing a Texan likes better than to brag about his heritage."

"I can't see you bragging about anything. Unless it's Sam, of course."

Lyn flinched as if he had struck her. "I am very proud of Sam," she responded, her tone formal.

"I'd say you have every right to be. By the way, was there a game this morning?" He took another swallow of his lemonade.

"Yes. Sam called to tell me the Owls won." In spite of her determination to remain aloof, Lyn's pride in her daughter shown through.

"Dad said he would like to see the team play again."

"They play at Kerrville next Saturday. The next home game will be in two weeks." Lyn watched Burne from the corner of her eye. His expression was thoughtful, and she wondered what he was thinking.

The conversation lagged.

"Lyn, would you have dinner with me one evening next week?"

Lyn's head flew around, and her blue eyes went wide with surprise.

When she didn't answer, Burne persisted. "I think we've been properly introduced," he teased.

"Thank you for asking but I don't date."

It was Burne's turn to look surprised. "You don't even go to dinner with a friend?"

"If you're referring to *male* friends, the answer is no." Lyn straightened in her chair, her back erect and both feet planted firmly on the floor.

"May I ask why?"

"First of all, I don't have any male friends and secondly, I'm not interested in that kind of friendship." Her tone said the subject was closed.

"You're a hard woman, Lyn DeVinney. How is a fellow going to convince you that having dinner with a *male* friend can be enjoyable?" Burne ignored her rejection.

"I don't think you can."

With a heart-stopping grin, he looked full into her face. "I don't give up that easily."

* * *

Theresa tapped Paul on the shoulder. "I hate to bother you, but have you seen Lyn? I need to talk with her."

Paul knew exactly where Theresa could find Lyn. He had been

watching her and MacKenzie as they relaxed with their drinks. He pointed to the opposite end of the patio.

"She's sitting over there with MacKenzie." A sly grin spread across his handsome face. Theresa was just the person to break up that cozy scene and, just maybe, give MacKenzie somebody else to think about.

As the young woman approached, Lyn came to her feet. The nursing unit was having its own party, and she knew Theresa would not seek her out unless it was an emergency.

Burne rose from his chair as the young woman stopped in front of them.

"I'm sorry to bother you, Lyn, but there's a problem with Mrs. Grimes. Can you come to the nursing unit?"

"Yes, of course. Theresa, this is Burne MacKenzie. His father is one of our residents. Burne, Theresa Martinez, our diet clerk."

"Hello, Theresa. I've heard a lot about you."

Theresa's dark eyes opened wide. "You have?"

Burne grinned, then explained, "I know your brother, Pete. He and I work on the same construction project."

Theresa smiled. "It's nice to meet you, Mr. MacKenzie."

"The pleasure is all mine," Burne told her.

"Excuse me, Burne. I need to check into this right away." Lyn hurried away, Theresa following on her heels.

CHAPTER FIVE

The flagstone patio was decked out for the festivities. Tables for four, six and eight were covered with red and white checked cloths. Bright, blue, plastic dinnerware and red and white napkins were stacked on one end of the buffet table. A clever centerpiece representing a bale of straw with a cowboy and his horse, a cow and her calf drew enthusiastic comments from the diners. Huge bowls of potato salad and coleslaw, chafing dishes of the ever-present staple—pinto beans—pickles, onions and other relishes filled the table to overflowing. A large watermelon had been scooped out and filled with a luscious assortment of fresh fruit. A smaller table held an array of tempting desserts: apple and pecan pie, and chocolate-iced brownies.

Burne, Lawrence, and the Schumanns filled their plates and returned to their table. "This is great," Burne exclaimed as he swallowed a mouthful of tasty barbecue.

Myra Schumann smiled at the young man she had known for most of his life. "Yes, you can't beat Texas barbecue! I think the food here is exceptionally good although I know Lawrence doesn't agree with me." She smiled fondly at the older MacKenzie. Myra was a plump matronly woman with a wealth of curly white hair.

Lawrence's answering smile was a bit sheepish. "Well, it has improved somewhat," he admitted grudgingly.

Burne listened to the exchange between his father and Myra with satisfaction. Yes, the Schumanns would help his father adjust. Myra and his mother had been best friends, and Joe was his father's favorite golf partner. Perhaps this move had not been a mistake after all.

It had occurred to Burne that the Schumanns might know something of Lyn's background, and he had been waiting for the right moment. The discussion of food at The Manor seemed like the opportune time.

"Dad gave Ms. DeVinney a hard time there for awhile," he remarked as he forked a bite of potato salad.

"So I hear," Joe affirmed. He was a big man with broad shoulders, and his thinning gray hair emphasized a ruddy complexion.

"Shame on you, Lawrence! Lyn is a fine young woman, and she does a very good job," Myra chastised, her brown eyes flashing with indignation.

Burne hesitated. *Oh, what the hell!* He had to find out. "She does seem very conscientious." He managed to keep his tone casual.

"Lyn is more than conscientious," Myra said emphatically. "She really cares about the residents and their well-being."

"I'm sure she does," Burne agreed.

"In spite of what some of them say, I admire her for the way she is raising her little girl."

"She is a single parent, isn't she?" Burne struggled to keep his voice neutral.

"Yes. I don't know much about the circumstances, Lyn is a very private person, but she doesn't have any contact with the child's father. Or, so the gossips say," Myra hastened to add.

"That hardly seems fair. I can't see a man being willing to give up all rights to his child." A frown wrinkled Burne's brow.

Myra looked directly at Burne, a grim look on her normally pleasant features. "No, but in cases like hers it's not all that unusual. He must be a perfect scoundrel, because she didn't marry him."

Burne felt as if he had been hit in the gut. He had assumed Lyn was divorced. No wonder she did not have or want male friends. He was not one to sit in judgment, but it made the situation more difficult. His problem would be to convince her to trust him, and he feared the task might be insurmountable.

✻ ✻ ✻

As they reached the nursing unit, Lyn turned to Theresa. "What is the problem?"

"Mrs. Grimes' formula isn't in the refrigerator in the nursing unit. I checked the kitchen, and it's not there either."

Her expression puzzled, Lyn replied, "Surely Gertrude made it up yesterday. It's not like her to forget."

"What should I do?"

"Let me double check to be sure it wasn't put someplace else. If we don't find it, see if you can get her to take a can of the supplement Dr. Hayden prescribed." Lyn stepped into the mini kitchen that served the nursing unit.

"What about tomorrow's feedings?" Theresa's pretty face reflected her concern.

"I'll make them up myself before I leave."

Theresa smiled. Lyn could always be counted on to solve a problem quickly and efficiently.

A tired Lyn locked the kitchen doors and started toward the employees' parking lot. It had been a long day, and the food service staff had left some time ago. The missing formula had not been found, and she had spent over an hour preparing new ones. She could hear the strains of country-western music coming from the patio and sighed. She loved to dance but opportunities were few. Her brother-in-law, Bob, one or two other male relatives and Charley did not provide many partners.

"Lyn, wait."

Lyn recognized Burne's voice before she turned to see him walking toward her.

"What happened? You never came back to the party."

"There was an emergency, and I had to do some work in the kitchen." Lyn took a deep breath, wishing she could just disappear. She knew her appearance was anything but attractive. Her skirt was wrinkled, and there were food stains on the front of her blouse.

"Aren't you coming back? I was hoping you would dance with me." He moved closer until they were standing mere inches apart.

Lyn caught the hopeful note in his voice and, in spite of her exhaustion, her heartbeat accelerated. Unbidden, a brief image of Kevin and his winning ways flashed through her mind. She could not let herself be interested in Burne MacKenzie. He would be gone in a short time, and she would be left with nothing but memories. Lyn shook her head. "No, I'm sorry, but I need to pick up Sam."

"I'll accept that—for now." His gray eyes drilled into her. "But I've already told you. I don't give up easily."

In spite of herself, Lyn smiled. "Like father, like son?"

Burne returned her smile with a heart-stopping grin. "I guess you could say that. Dad can be pretty determined, as you know."

"Yes, he can." Turning toward her car, she added, "I really do need to go, Burne. Janet and Charley have had Sam all day."

"I understand. Good night, Lyn."

"Good night."

As she drove away, Lyn's thoughts were filled with Burne MacKenzie. What was she going to do about his persistent efforts to break down her resistance?

* * *

Dangling his legs in the cool blue water of the indoor pool, Burne was glad Andy had urged him to join the health club. After a hot day at the construction site with its myriad problems, a relaxing swim was just what he needed. He had done a couple of slow laps just to unwind and felt his energy building up. Most of the swimmers were men like him, in a job where physical activity was limited. He was lucky he wasn't cooped up inside all the time but expediting materials and settling labor disputes did not require much physical exertion.

A flash of bright blue spandex and a pair of long legs caught Burn's eye just as they disappeared into the water. The man surfaced and rapidly swam the length of the pool, turned and repeated the process. Pausing a few seconds to catch his breath, he swam in Burn's direction. He reached shallow water and stood up, his body sleek and tanned with the look of an athlete. Burne's eyes narrowed as he took in the man's blond hair, darker now from being wet, broad shoulders and classic features. There was something vaguely familiar about him, but Burne couldn't remember where he had seen him.

"Hello, Mr. MacKenzie. I didn't know you belonged to the club," his smile was a dazzling white.

"I'm afraid you have the advantage, Mr…"

"Mansfield. Paul Mansfield. I'm the chef at The Hill Country Manor."

Burne felt the other man's appraisal and knew he measured up pretty well. He was well muscled, and there was no hint of a spare tire around his middle. His long legs were well developed and covered with the same sandy hair as his chest. Burne believed in keeping in shape.

"Yes, I remember now. You were at the barbecue. And, by the way, the meal was delicious. You Texans really know how to cook a side of beef."

"Thanks. I should confess, though. I'm not a Texan. Not a native, anyway. I'm from California."

That accounted for the golden look Burne recognized. Probably spent a lot of time under a sun lamp. "Well, you certainly picked up their secrets."

"Thanks, again," Paul grinned. He climbed out of the water and settled himself beside Burne. "Is your father getting adjusted to living at The Manor?"

Burne grinned, thinking Paul probably had been involved in some of the adjustments. "Yes, I think so. Especially now that Joe and Myra are back."

"The Schumanns? I saw you together at the barbecue."

"They were our neighbors in Indiana. Their son, Scott and I went to school together."

"They're originally from San Antonio, aren't they?" Paul asked, as he splashed the water with his feet.

"Yes, Joe was transferred to Indiana by his company when the kids were in grade school. It was hard for them at first, but they knew they would come back to Texas when Joe retired."

Striving to keep his tone casual, Burne changed the subject. "What about you? How long have you worked at The Manor?"

"A little over two years."

"Isn't it unusual for a professional chef to work in a place like that?" Burne leaned back, resting his weight on his palms, trying to give the impression he was making idle conversation.

"No, not really. The more exclusive places have them."

"I wasn't aware of that. Seems like there would be more money at a fancy restaurant or a big hotel."

"There is some difference in salary, but there are other compensations from working in a place like The Manor." Paul replied, his tone defensive.

Burne felt his gut tighten. Was one of those compensations Lyn DeVinney? "I'm sure there are. Do you work directly under Ms. DeVinney?"

"Yes. Lyn is responsible for the entire food service operation including the nursing unit."

"That's a lot of responsibility, but she seems to know her job." Burne was watching the expression on Paul's face from the corner of his eye.

"She does and she's good at it, too."

Burne turned to Paul with an easy grin, and asked, "Then you're not one of those *macho* men who don't like working for a woman?"

Paul's expression was serious when he replied. "I'd rather work for Lyn than a lot of men I've known."

Burn's eyebrows raised a notch.

Paul continued, "Lyn is one of the most honest people I've ever met. She bends over backwards to be fair and is always willing to give you the benefit of the doubt. She gives credit when it's due, too. If Lyn has a fault, it's her dedication to her job. She would probably live at The Manor if it weren't for Sam. She is Lyn's one weakness, as far as I know."

Burne caught the barest hint of criticism in Paul's comment that Lyn might be overly involved with her daughter. Aha! He seemed unduly opinionated concerning his superior.

"I guess she just wants to be a good mother. Sometimes mothers who work have guilt feelings about it. I know my sister did. When she had her second child, she quit. Of course, by that time my brother-in-law

A TASTE OF TEXAS

was earning good money so it wasn't necessary for her to work." Burne came to Lyn's defense.

"You're probably right. Anyway, I'd better finish up here. I'm meeting a friend later. Nice talking with you, Mr. MacKenzie. I'm sure we'll be seeing each other again soon."

"I'm sure we will," Burne called after him as Paul slipped into the water and swam away.

Burne reflected on the conversation concerning Lyn and Sam. His gut instinct told him Paul had more interest in Lyn than he should have for the woman who was his boss.

* * *

The mystery of the missing formula had been solved. Gertrude, the diet aide responsible for the special diets in the nursing unit, readily admitted she must have overlooked preparing it.

"You don't know how bad I feel, Lyn! Poor Mrs. Grimes, being so helpless and all."

The woman was genuinely upset when she learned of the oversight, but her honesty in confessing her mistake was more important to Lyn than administering severe discipline.

"I know it wasn't deliberate, Gertrude. You're much too conscientious to have neglected your responsibility, but I do have to make a notation in your file."

"I understand. After all, I made a terrible mistake." The woman shifted uncomfortably in her chair.

The incident was duly recorded, but Lyn doubted it would occur again.

Lyn took the new menu printouts from her desk drawer. Her thoughts strayed to the barbecue and Burne MacKenzie. He had asked her out, she refused, he asked her to dance, and again she refused.

Although he had said he was not giving up, she wondered if he would try again. Was he persevering because she turned him down? Was his ego bruised or was he really interested in her? Once or twice since Sam was born, she had been tempted to accept an invitation to dinner, but a mental image of Kevin and his smooth delivery always managed to stifle her desire. It had been she and Sam for so long, Lyn knew she would encounter problems should she suddenly display an interest in a social life that did not include her daughter.

"Do you have a minute?"

Abruptly startled from her reverie, Lyn focused blankly on Paul's tanned features. He was standing in the doorway, a clipboard in his hand.

"Yes, of course. Come in, Paul." She mentally scolded herself for daydreaming.

He walked into the room and seated himself in a chair across from her desk. "We need to make some substitutions in next week's menus."

"What do we need to change?"

"I haven't been able to get the kiwis for the fruit plates or the bib lettuce we need, and there seems to be a shortage of lamb."

Lyn sighed. For some reason, ordinary problems seem to require more effort to solve. "If you can't locate the kiwi from another vendor, we'll just have to go with melon, pineapple and strawberries."

Paul made a notation on his clipboard.

Lyn was silent for a moment, and then continued. "Do what you can about the bib lettuce and a substitute. I know the shortage has driven the price through the roof. As for lamb, maybe you can locate some veal."

Again Paul nodded and made notes.

When he made no effort to leave, Lyn inquired, "Is there anything else?"

"That about takes care of it. By the way, I ran into Burne MacKenzie at the health club the other night."

Lyn's eyes widened and her expression altered slightly. "Is he a member?" Her voice was deliberately casual.

"Yeah. He was at the pool. Evidently, he likes to swim. Said it helps him unwind. I didn't ask him what his job is, but he probably doesn't get much exercise."

"I really don't know what he does. His father said he's a field representative. Something to do with union negotiations, I think." Lyn toyed with her pen, making idle doodles on the pad in front of her.

"Ugh! I don't envy him. From what I know about it, and that's not much, that kind of business can get ugly." Distaste marred his handsome features.

"I suppose so, but evidently he knows what he's doing or he wouldn't be doing it." Lyn felt compelled to defend Burne.

"He's no dummy, that's for sure," he said, rising from his chair. When Lyn offered no response, he turned and left the room.

She stared at the unfinished menus while the conversation with Paul repeated itself in her mind. It was strange that Burne chose the same health club Paul belonged to, but then she remembered it was one of the few with an indoor pool. She wondered if Paul knew Burne had asked her out, and she had turned him down. It was not likely since she had not mentioned it to anyone at The Manor. Surely Burne would not confide in Paul hoping to learn more about her. There was nothing Paul could tell Burne about her private life. He knew about Sam, she had never made a secret of the child's illegitimacy, but outside of her family, nobody knew the ugly details.

She pictured Burne's clear gray eyes as he told her, "I don't give up easily." What would he think if he knew the truth? Would those eyes turn smoky with pity? Would his sensuous lips curl in disgust? Did he see her as a woman he wanted only to lure into his bed? Lyn shivered as if a cold wind had touched her. Not since Kevin had she let a man get so close to her. Burne MacKenzie had penetrated her defenses and she was terrified.

Texas Barbecued Brisket

Serves 10

1 trimmed brisket (5-6 pounds with a layer of fat at
least ¼ inch thick)
3 tablespoons chili powder
1 tablespoon coarse salt
2 teaspoons black pepper
1 ½ teaspoons brown sugar
1 ½ teaspoons garlic salt
1 ½ teaspoons onion powder
1 teaspoon ground cumin
1 teaspoon dried oregano
½-1 teaspoon cayenne pepper

Vinegar-Beer Mop Sauce *
1 cup distilled white vinegar
1 cup beer
1 tablespoon garlic salt
1 tablespoon brown sugar
1 teaspoon hot red pepper flakes
1 teaspoon black pepper

Rinse the brisket under cold running water and blot dry with paper
towels. Combine all the ingredients for the rub in a small bowl and stir
to mix. Rub this mixture into the brisket and onto all sides. Let the
brisket stand in the refrigerator for 4 to 6 hours.

Combine all the ingredients for the mop sauce in a non-reactive
bowl and stir until the salt and brown sugar are dissolved.

Set up the grill and preheat to low.

Place the brisket, fat side up, in an aluminum foil pan and place in the center of the grill. Grill the brisket about 6 hours or until tender. Baste or mop the brisket with the mop sauce once per hour for the first 4 hours. To test for doneness, use an instant-read meat thermometer. The internal temperature should be about 190 degrees F.

Transfer the brisket to a cutting board and let rest for 10 minutes. Thinly slice across the grain, using a sharp knife. Transfer the sliced meat to a platter and pour the juices on top.

* Or use your favorite bottled sauce or recipe

Cowpoke Beans

1 pound pinto beans
2 ½ cups cold water
½ pound bacon (ham or meat scraps may be used)
dried red chili pepper
medium onion, chopped
1 clove garlic, minced
1 can (6 oz.) tomato paste
1 ½ tablespoons chili powder
1 teaspoon salt
1 teaspoon cumin
½ teaspoon marjoram

Put beans and water into Dutch oven. Bring to a boil. Reduce heat and simmer for one hour. Stir in remaining ingredients. Cover and simmer for 3 hours until tender. Add more water if necessary. Adjust seasonings as desired.

Texas Pecan Pie

1 unbaked 9 inch pie shell
1 egg white, lightly beaten
3 eggs
1 cup light corn syrup
1/3 cup butter, melted
1 teaspoon vanilla
dash salt
1 cup pecans

With a pastry brush, brush inside of pie shell with egg white. Set aside to dry at room temperature for at least one hour. Preheat oven to 350 degrees. In a large mixer bowl at low speed, beat eggs, corn syrup, brown sugar, butter, vanilla and salt until well blended. Pour into crust; sprinkle pecans evenly over the top. With the back of a spoon, press pecans into the filling to coat and keep evenly spread over the top. Bake for 45 to 50 minutes or until filling is set and pastry is nicely browned. Cool on wire rack for 2 ½ to 3 hours before serving. Refrigerate leftovers.

CHAPTER SIX

Burne checked the printout for the third time. The result was the same. There were definitely some materials missing. He made a mental note to discuss it with Andy. As if his thoughts had conjured up the project engineer, Andy slammed the door shut.

"Damn that infernal wind! I don't see how those guys stay up there." He tossed his hard hat on the desk.

Burne grinned at the man's windblown appearance. His dark hair was standing up in all directions, and his khaki slacks were wrapped around his legs like bandages. Burne had worked with Andy on several jobs, and they were good friends. "They're used to it. Pete says they don't even notice it."

"Lucky them!"

"Andy, we have a problem." Burne's voice was grim.

Andy's brown eyes widened. "Let me phone Shelley first. I promised to take her out to dinner if she could find a sitter, and I'll need to make reservations." Andy and Shelley were the parents of a two-year old toddler.

While Andy was on the phone, Burne let his thoughts stray to Lyn. He had not seen her since the barbecue, but he would rectify that matter soon. His father had expressed an interest in going to the ball game on Saturday.

"What's going on?"

Andy broke into Burne's thoughts, and he forced his mind away from Lyn to the problem at hand. He handed Andy the print out. "I've checked the inventory three times. There's some pilfering going on. Not much, but every check shows a little more discrepancy."

"Do you think it's an inside job?" Andy studied the figures.

"I don't see how it could be anything else. There's never been any sign of forced entry." Burne stood up and rubbed the back of his neck. He had been sitting at the computer all morning.

"Have you talked with Dan about it?"

Dan Potts was superintendent for Williams Bohrn and responsible for all materials delivered and stored on the site although he assigned tasks to others.

"No, but we need to."

"Let me keep my eyes open for a few days. I'm around the men more than you are. I may be able to pick up something."

"O.K. Let's wait a couple of days before we say anything to Dan." Burne went back to the computer.

The door opened with a bang and Manuel stepped into the office. "Hey you should try Rosa's for lunch today. She's got a' enchilada special, and you know Rosa's enchiladas!"

Burne and Andy exchanged glances. Was Manuel involved in the missing inventory? As timekeeper, he had keys to the office but not the sheds where the materials were kept. With a slight shake of his head, Burne turned to answer. "Yeah, I sure do. That's where I'm heading. How about you, Andy?"

"I'll pass. Shelley got a sitter, and we're going out so I don't want to eat a heavy lunch."

"Want me to bring you something?"

"Yeah, thanks. A roast beef on wheat or whatever she has."

As Burne finished his iced tea and waited for Andy's sandwich, he mentally reviewed the problem of the missing inventory. Supplies and tools were difficult to keep track of, and small thefts went unnoticed until the discrepancy became obvious. There had been incidents on other jobs and, with one exception, the thefts were instigated by dishonest employees.

Andy had seen nothing unusual when he came into the office after the shift ended. "I hung around after the men clocked out, and they all left within a few minutes of one another. They didn't seem to congregate in a group or anything." He began to clear his desk.

"It's too soon to expect a break, Andy. We'll just have to keep on our toes."

"Time for me to get out of here. Shelley will be all dressed up and rarin' to go."

"Are you taking her some place special?" Burne leaned back in his chair. It had been a trying day.

"You bet! The Old San Francisco Steakhouse. She wants to see "The Girl in the Red Velvet Swing." I have to admit, I'm rather looking forward to that myself." Andy's grin was just short of lecherous.

Burne gave a low whistle. "I've heard a lot about the place."

"Maybe we should have made it a foursome." His look completely innocent, he asked, "Have you met anyone yet?"

Burne grinned. Andy liked to keep track of his romantic encounters. He and Shelley had tried to play Cupid on more than one occasion.

"You don't think I'd tell you if I have, do you?"

"No, I suppose not. But if you do, we expect to meet her."

"How could I forget?"

Andy guffawed, threw up his hand and hurried out the door.

Burne had not told Andy about Lyn, because the situation was too unsettled. He did not want to reveal Lyn's background. *Hell*, he did not know the facts himself and, until he convinced her to go out with him, it was better that Andy did not know about her.

* * *

The interrogation room with its scarred wooden table and chairs held a faint odor of stale smoke. Burne surveyed the three men grouped near the window overlooking the alley. The patrolmen who had been hired as security guards, and their sergeant were speaking in low tones. Burne felt Andy nudge his elbow.

"What are they waiting for? I need to get back to the job site." Patience was not one of Andy's virtues.

"They said something about the head honcho, Frank Parker."

As if in answer to Burne's comment, the door opened and a well-dressed man of middle age entered the room.

"Sorry I kept you waiting, gentlemen, but there was an emergency that needed my attention. Please be seated."

Burne had met Parker when he made a courtesy call at the job site. Burne and Andy were well acquainted with the patrolmen, Tom Schneider and Juan Mendoza. The only introduction necessary was that of Sergeant Matt Soliz. He was a short stocky man with a thick black mustache.

Parker took a seat at the head of the table and spread a set of folders in front of him. Burne and Andy sat on his right while his men took chairs on the left. Burne wondered if he was following some kind of protocol.

Opening one of the folders, Parker took charge of the meeting.

"Now, let's get down to business. When did you first notice the discrepancies in your inventory?"

"The figures haven't tallied for several weeks, but the difference was so slight, I let it ride. We have a built in margin that allows for missing or lost materials," Burne explained. He had a folder of printouts in front of him.

"But the discrepancies have absorbed your margin, is that it?" Parker's eyes behind gold-rimmed glasses had narrowed, and he focused his gaze on Burne.

"In a nutshell."

Parker turned to the two patrolmen. "Tom, Juan, I've looked over your reports. No mention of unauthorized personnel on the site after hours, no sign of forced entry, nothing out of the ordinary."

"No sir. I make my rounds on a regular basis, but I haven't seen or heard anything unusual," Schneider confirmed. He was a slender man of medium height with brown hair and eyes.

Mendoza had nothing to add to Tom's report.

"Looks like it's time for SAPD to step in," Parker stated.

"We don't have any choice," Burne agreed. "Whoever the culprits are, they have access to the sheds. If they were lifting the stuff in the daytime, they would have already been caught."

Parker's gaze traveled around the table and came to rest on Burne. "Not necessarily. Sometimes it's safer to overlook what's going on."

Burne's eyes narrowed, and he chose his words carefully. "At the present time, there are only three Williams Bohrn men from out of state, and we've all been with the company for a long time. All of the other employees are local men."

Parker closed the folder. "We'll get the investigation under way at once. I'll assign a couple of men to talk with the workers."

Burne stood up. "Tell your men to check with Dan Potts, the superintendent."

* * *

The ball hit the bat with a resounding crack and went soaring into left field. Sam took off running and quickly rounded the bases before sliding into home plate. The crowd was on its feet cheering, and Lyn felt the beginning of a headache. There was a large turn out for the game between the Mt. Laurel Owls and the Austin Ravens. It had been nip and tuck throughout the game and, with Sam's home run, the Owls led five to four.

Burne had turned up for the game with his father and the Schumanns in tow. Though he managed to seat himself next to Lyn, there had been no opportunity for a private conversation.

Lyn felt the touch of rough fingertips on her arm and looked up to see Burne grinning at her. He pointed to the field and mouthed, "She's a great player."

Lyn smiled at him, her pride in her daughter shining in her face. She felt the heat of his touch and withdrew her hand.

"We have to talk," he muttered in her ear.

Eyes wide, she stared at him. He kept his gaze leveled on her as he waited for her response. She shook her head and whispered, "No." Her stomach felt hollow and her headache intensified.

"Yes," he answered emphatically.

The umpire called a strike and the game was over; Owls five, Ravens, four. The crowd began to swarm onto the field. Janet yelled over her shoulder, "See you later," as she and Charley joined the celebration.

There was an awkward silence for a minute, then Myra came to Lyn's side and hugged her. "I'm so glad the Owls won. I know you're very proud of Sam and well you should be."

"Thank you, Mrs. Schumann." Lyn had difficulty concentrating. Burne was standing close, and she felt the warmth from his body as the crowd pressed them together.

"Give Sam my congratulations," Joe boomed above the noise.

"I will, thank you," she replied as she tried to collect her thoughts. Her head was throbbing. "I'm sorry, but I must get down on the field. Sam will be looking for me."

Her smile strained, she hurried away.

Burne watched as Lyn vanished in the crowd. He did not notice Myra's speculative look as he pondered how to overcome Lyn's refusal to talk with him. There had to be a way.

"Are you ready to go, son?" Lawrence asked, his voice impatient.

"Yes. How about you two?" Burne turned to the Schumanns.

"Yes," Myra answered. "Thank you for bringing us, Burne. We enjoyed watching the girls play. Lyn seemed appreciative, too."

"I'm sure she is." He followed his father and the Schumanns from the bleachers.

* * *

As he pulled the Suburban into the space next to Lyn's red Cavalier, Burne's nerves were strung as tight as a barbed wire fence. He had lain awake half the night trying to figure out a way to get her alone. He knew she would not go out with him, and he doubted she would even let him buy her a cup of coffee at a nearby restaurant. Finally in the wee hours, he decided to go for broke. He left work early, drove out to the Manor and waited until she left for the day.

Burne watched the back door in the rear view mirror. Lord, he felt foolish. Here he was, a grown man sneaking around like a teenager. The door opened and Lyn came out. She paused, looking at the Suburban parked next to her, then walked briskly toward it. As she neared the parked cars, Burne got out of the vehicle and stood with his back against the door. His eyes surveyed her slender figure. She was wearing a tailored blue dress instead of her usual skirt and blouse. He imagined how the color of the dress emphasized the blue of her eyes. As she approached, he saw the determined expression on her face. He had his work cut out for him.

Without giving her a chance to speak, he told her, "I couldn't think of any other way to talk with you."

"Hello, Burne," she ignored his explanation and started toward the driver's side of her car.

He stepped away from the Suburban and put his hand on her arm. "Lyn, at least give me a chance."

She hesitated, chewing her lower lip, her blue eyes meeting his gray ones. "There's nothing to talk about."

"I think there is. You know I'm attracted to you or I wouldn't be standing here trying to convince you to go out with me."

"I told you. I don't date."

"I know that. And I told *you* I don't give up easily. Good Lord, Lyn, let's go someplace where we can get out of this heat and have some privacy. I feel like an illicit lover standing here." The minute the words were out of his mouth, Burne knew he had said the wrong thing.

Lyn's face went from pink to white. She jerked her arm free and, with a look that would have frozen an Eskimo, she turned her back on him. She fumbled for her keys, found them and unlocked the car door.

What could he say? How was he going to get out of this one? If he apologized, then she would know he had found out about her past. Her past? *Damn!* He didn't care about her past. It was her future he was interested in.

"Lyn, wait."

She released the door handle, turned to look at him. "All right. Do you know where the Dairy Bar is?"

An expression of relief came over Burne's face and he nodded.

Burne followed Lyn and pulled in beside her. He locked the vehicle, and they walked toward the building.

"I don't have much time, Burne. I have to pick up Sam."

When his eyebrows raised, she explained, "She stays at Janet's in the afternoon after school. When school is out, she goes to a morning day camp. I don't want Sam to be a latch-key kid."

"I agree with you there. It's good you have a friend who is willing to help out."

"Yes, it is."

Burne held the door, and they entered the restaurant. It was nearly empty.

"What would you like?" he asked, reaching for his wallet.

"A diet coke will be fine. It's too hot for coffee."

Seated, with tall frosty drinks before them, Burne searched for an opening. What could he say? He'd already told her he was attracted to her. Taking a deep breath, he plunged in.

"I know you don't date, and it's none of my business why you haven't. I'm interested in *now*. Why won't you consider having dinner with me? If you're worried about my character or anything else about me, I'm sure Joe and Myra will vouch for me. After all, they've known me a long time." He grinned, his gray eyes twinkling. "They can tell you all about the stunts Larry and Scott and I pulled in high school."

"Larry?"

Burne's merry expression altered and his eyes held a hint of sadness. "Larry was my older brother. He was killed in an automobile accident five years ago."

"I'm sorry." Lyn's blue eyes reflected genuine sympathy.

Burne nodded. The loss was still painful.

"Scott lives in El Paso, doesn't he?" Lyn changed the subject.

His long fingers caressed the damp paper cup. "Yes. General Motors sent him to work in their plant in Mexico after he graduated from the Institute. He studied engineering so it was logical he would go to work for G.M."

Burne kept the conversation light, hoping Lyn would relax. "Our families always hoped Scott and Annie would marry some day, but she said he was too much like a brother to her."

"Annie is your sister, isn't she?"

"Yes, my kid sister. She did pick a fine man, though. Steve is a lawyer and a very good one."

"The Schumanns have a daughter in New York, don't they?"

Burne knew Lyn wanted to keep the conversation away from herself, but he would play along and see what developed.

"Yes, her name is Christina. Her husband is with AT&T. She and Annie both went to Indiana University."

"Where did you go to school?" she asked as she sipped her cola.

"Purdue." He indicated the monogram on the pocket of his white knit shirt.

Lyn peered at the black and gold letters.

"I majored in business administration with a minor in construction technology. How about you?"

"I did my undergraduate work at Incarnate Word." Lyn smoothed out the fold in her napkin and refolded it.

"That's in San Antonio, isn't it?"

"Yes. They have a good dietetic program."

"What about your graduate degree? Where did you go for that?" Burne looked at her over the top of his cup.

Lyn took a deep breath before she answered. "I did my internship at Kansas State and stayed on to get a master's." Her voice was emotionless, and she kept her eyes focused on the wood-grain tabletop.

"I joined the Air Force right out of college and, when my tour was up, I went to work for Williams Bohrn. I took some labor relations courses before I went into the field." Burne finished his drink and set the cup aside.

"Sounds like you've traveled a lot." Lyn toyed with her straw.

"Yes, I've enjoyed it, but it's not as exciting as it sounds."

"I haven't traveled very much, but I hope to do more now that Sam is old enough to appreciate it. And speaking of Sam, I really need to get over to Janet's." She pushed back her chair.

"Thank you for spending this time with me, Lyn. Please say you'll let me take you out to dinner soon."

"I've enjoyed it too, Burne. As for dinner, I don't think so."

Burne's expression mirrored his disappointment. His brow furrowed, then suddenly he grinned. "I have an idea. Why don't you let me take you and Sam some place for the day? Fiesta Texas or Sea World, maybe."

Lyn smiled. "Sam does love Sea World."

"At least say you'll think about it," he coaxed, his eyes dark with feeling.

"All right. I'll talk it over with Sam. That's the best I can do."

"That's great! For now."

CHAPTER SEVEN

Lyn waited several days before telling Sam about Burne's invitation to Sea World.

"No, Sam, you don't have to go. But I don't think you're being quite fair. Mr. MacKenzie has invited us because I told him you enjoyed going there." Lyn washed the greens for the salad while Sam set the table for dinner.

"But, Mom, why would he want to take us? We don't even know him."

Lyn fumbled for an answer. How could she explain that Burne was interested in her, and that he wouldn't take no for an answer? She certainly could not tell Sam he was wearing down her resistance.

"That's not exactly true, Sam. You've met him and he came to two of your games. He visits his father often and we've talked quite a bit."

Sam looked at her mother, her face shaping into a frown. "Okay," Sam nodded. "When are we going?"

Lyn gave an inward sigh of relief. The first hurdle had been overcome. "I don't know yet. Since you have ball games every Saturday for the next few weeks, we will have to go on Sunday. I'll discuss it with Burne."

Lyn had an opportunity to talk with Burne when he visited his father the next evening. She was leaving her office when he came hurrying down the hall. Her heartbeat speeded up as she recognized his tall form. She admitted Burne MacKenzie had a definite effect on her emotions.

"I'm glad I caught you," he called out, his voice a bit breathless. "Do we have a date for Sea World?"

"Yes." Lyn smiled as she watched a grin crease Burne's features.

"Great! When can we go?" His silver eyes fastened themselves on her blue ones.

"How about Sunday afternoon? We get home from church about noon. We could meet you there to save time." Lyn had a hunch Sam would like that idea, but she was not going to insist.

"Nothing doing. I'll pick you up at your apartment." Burne's tone left no room for argument.

"Actually, I think it would be best."

"Are you staying for dinner?" She changed the subject.

"Yes, I think Dad could use the company, and I need to put a good meal under my belt."

His grin told her that good nutrition was not a priority with him. *I could change all that.* Lyn realized where her thoughts were leading and mentally chastised herself. *You're not responsible for the entire population.*

"I think you'll find something you like on the menu. And speaking of food, I need to be getting home. I promised Sam hamburgers for dinner." Lyn fished in her purse for her car keys.

"I'm really looking forward to Sunday. I'll pick you up at one o'clock, if that's O.K.?" Burne stepped back.

"That's fine. I'm looking forward to it, too. Good night." Lyn turned toward the back parking lot as Burne, his expression thoughtful, watched her walk away.

Lyn changed her slacks for the third time. Scrutinizing her reflection in the mirror, she nodded. Yes, the white poplin looked much better with the red knit shirt than the navy or beige ones. Fastening gold hoops in her ears, she surveyed her make-up. A light touch of foundation that contained sunscreen, a hint of blush, taupe eye shadow, charcoal liner and soft black mascara applied that morning needed little repair. She touched up her lipstick and ran a comb through her hair. That should do it.

She tried to ignore the butterflies flitting around in the pit of her stomach. Sam had been dressed and waiting for several minutes while Lyn made up her mind. The doorbell chimed and her heart skipped a beat. She took a deep breath and exhaled slowly.

"Mom, he's here," Sam yelled from the living room.

Lyn hurried from the bedroom and opened the door to see Burne smiling at her. Wearing a navy blue knit shirt, his silver gray eyes were startling in his tanned face. Lyn's pulse fluttered, then speeded up as she caught the scent of his cologne. It was a clean, outdoor fragrance that made her think of pine trees and clear mountain streams. With an effort, she brought her thoughts back into focus.

"Hello, Burne. Won't you come in?"

Burne stepped inside and Lyn closed the door. There was an awkward pause and she hastened to fill it. "You've met Sam."

"Hello, Mr. MacKenzie," Sam dutifully greeted him.

"Hello, Sam. I don't think we need to be so formal. Why don't you call me Burne?"

"Okay," Sam agreed but her voice lacked any sign of enthusiasm.

"Please sit down, Burne. Would you like something to drink? I have iced tea or soda." She turned toward the kitchen.

"No, thanks."

"I guess we had better go, then. There may be a big crowd at the gate." Lyn picked up her purse while Sam headed out the door.

As he walked Lyn and Sam to their door, Burne reflected on the events of the afternoon. There had been moments when he was able to talk with Lyn alone, but they were few in number. First, they had gone to see Shamu perform, and Sam insisted on sitting at the edge of the splash zone. He had walked around half of the afternoon with his pants spotted and clinging to his legs. Lyn managed to avoid some of the spray but both of them had gotten wet. Then, as if the whales hadn't done enough damage, the playful dolphins added insult to injury. Looking down at his wrinkled clothing, Burne grinned. What a man would not do to spend time with a pretty woman.

Sam reached the apartment first, carrying the booty she had accumulated. She had reluctantly allowed Burne to buy her a stuffed replica of Shamu while Lyn invested in a tee shirt proclaiming Sea World to be San Antonio's most popular tourist attraction.

"I've enjoyed today, Burne. Thank you for taking us." Lyn searched in her purse for her keys.

"I enjoyed it too, Lyn. I hope Sam had a good time." His voice held a note of skepticism.

Lyn's face colored a delicate pink. Sam had not been rude to Burne, but it was plain she had not accepted his friendship. "I'm sure she did. This situation is new to her. We've never gone anyplace except with family or close friends. I hope you understand."

"I do. She's a fine little girl. Don't worry about it."

They had reached the entrance to the building and Lyn handed Sam her key ring. "Go on up, Sam. I'll be there in a few minutes."

Sam eyed first her mother, then Burne. She frowned, but her voice was polite when she said, "Thank you for taking me to Sea World, Mr. Mac . . Burne. I enjoyed it very much."

"You're welcome, Sam," Burne grinned, his tone casual.

Sam, jingling the keys in her hand, turned toward the door. Throwing a backward glance over her shoulder, she told Burne goodbye.

The apartment complex was built around an open courtyard. Taking Lyn's elbow, Burne steered her in the direction of a park bench sitting under a live oak tree. She looked up to protest and he stopped abruptly, causing her to stumble. He grabbed her shoulder with his free hand, and she was caught in the circle of his arms. Lyn's body went rigid and she stood perfectly still. Her face was pale, and her blue eyes were staring at him with something akin to fear. Good Lord, did she think he was going to attack her?

"Lyn, what is it?" There was concern in his voice, but he did not release her.

She swallowed painfully and tried to pull away.

Burne immediately dropped his arms. "I'm sorry. I thought you were going to fall."

"Thank...thank you. I did lose my balance for a minute." She sat down on the bench.

Burne watched her closely. Her nose was a bit shiny and she had chewed off most of her lipstick, but she was still the prettiest woman he knew. She looked up at him. Their eyes met and clung. *A man could drown in those deep blue pools.* His voice was ragged when he spoke. "Just sit still a minute and try to relax." Tearing his eyes away, he joined her on the bench.

The color was returning to her face. He waited, trying to organize his thoughts, then told her, "I enjoyed being with you and Sam today. Will you go out to dinner with me soon?"

Although he was sitting close beside her, he made no effort to touch her. "I'll think about it."

Burne released a pent up breath, and it whispered softly through his lips.

Lyn favored him with a gentle smile as she turned to him and added, "Why don't you call me next week?"

* * *

The waitresses were setting up the dining room for the dinner crowd. Pink tablecloths, white china with a thin blue trim, sparkling crystal and shining flatware added to the room's elegance. The carpet in a deep berry shade contrasted with antique white walls, slate blue wood trim and blue, pink and white striped draperies. A profusion of green plants in brass and ceramic containers were artfully scattered about.

Lyn stepped into the flurry of activity with an armload of pink napkins. "These are fresh from the laundry. I'll help fold them." One of the waitresses had called in sick, and Lyn knew an extra pair of hands was always welcome. She dropped the stack on an uncovered table and sat down to concentrate on the intricate style she preferred. The muted ringing of the telephone in her office interrupted her.

Picking it up in mid-ring she answered, her voice a bit breathless, "Dining Services, Lyn DeVinney."

"Hello, Lyn. This is Burne."

As if he had to identify himself. She would recognize that rich masculine voice anywhere. He had told her he would call her, and she admitted she had been waiting to hear from him.

"Hello, Burne. How are you?"

"I'm fine. And you?"

"Just fine, thank you." Lyn knew she sounded stiff and formal. She sat down in one of the chairs facing her desk.

"I'm driving out to see Dad this evening, but I was afraid I'd miss you. Do you realize I don't have your home number?"

"Oh. It's unlisted, but I'll give it to you."

"Let me grab a pen and something to write on." There was a slight pause. "Shoot."

She gave him the number.

"Got it," he repeated it. "Now, how about dinner Saturday night?"

Lyn hesitated. She had agonized over her decision for several days. Her secret heart admitted she wanted to see him, but her common sense told her she would be making a mistake.

"Lyn, are you still there?"

"Yes."

"I'm going to tell it like it is, Lyn. You know I have feelings for you, but if you don't want to go out alone with me, just tell me and I won't bother you again." Burne's voice was firm.

As if he were standing before her, a vision of Burne's face appeared. The clear gray of his yes darkened to a stormy hue, and his strong jaw and chin were set in stern lines. Then his lips curled in a sensuous smile, and the fine lines around his eyes crinkled. Yes, he was definitely an interesting man. Couldn't her practical self bend just a little? Did she want her life to be completely void of entertainment? Suddenly, as if a wall had crumbled, Lyn felt her emotions tumble free. She gripped the phone tightly, took a deep breath and said, "Yes, I'd like to have dinner with you."

"That's great! Is Saturday night okay?"

Lyn swallowed her trepidation and replied, "Yes."

"Is there any place special you'd like to go?"

"No, not really. I'll let you pick the place."

"I don't know very much about the city, but I'll check a few places out. What time should I pick you up?"

"Since it takes about thirty minutes to drive into San Antonio, is seven o'clock too early?"

"No, that's fine with me. I'm looking forward to it. Goodbye, Lyn."

Lyn agonized all evening how to tell Sam she was going out with Burne on Saturday night. She needed to line up a sitter, and she had no idea where to start. It had never been a problem before since Sam usually stayed at Cathy's when Lyn went out. This was different. She did not want to discuss her date with Janet. The Gruen family from church lived in the complex, and their daughter was in high school. Perhaps she would like to earn some extra money.

Sam had books and papers spread all over the dining table. Her dark head was bent, and she was writing diligently in a ruled notebook. At the sound of her mother's footsteps, she dropped the pencil and leaned back in her chair. "Boy, this stuff is hard! I don't see why we have to learn about all the little old countries in the world. I'll probably never go to any of them," she complained.

Lyn smiled and ruffled her daughter's shiny brown hair. "Even if you never do, you still need to know about them. How about a break? You've been working hard all evening."

Sam nodded in agreement and jumped up from the table while Lyn took two sodas from the refrigerator. She settled herself on the sofa and patted the place beside her. "I have something to tell you."

Sam took a long drink from her can of soda. "What's up, Mom?"

Feeling the tension in her body tighten even more, Lyn took a deep breath and exhaled slowly. "I have accepted a dinner invitation from Burne for Saturday night."

Sam choked on a swallow of soda. Her eyes teared and she coughed. Lyn patted her lightly on the back. "Oh, Mom, do we have to go?"

"No, *you* don't have to go. This is a grown-up dinner. I'm going to ask Lisa Gruen to stay with you while I'm out."

Her brown eyes wide and her mouth agape, Sam looked at Lyn as if she had suddenly sprouted horns. When she finally found her voice, it was squeaky with shock. "You mean you have a *date?*"

Lyn's face colored to the roots of her hair, but she looked straight at Sam and replied, "Yes, I guess you could call it that."

"But…you never…well, it's always been just you and me. How come you're going out with *him?*"

"Don't you like Burne, Sam?"

"Oh, he's all right, I guess. But I just don't think we need a man hangin' around." Sam lowered her eyes and placed her empty soda bottle on the coffee table.

"I wouldn't say Burne is hanging around, as you put it." Lyn hated her tendency to sound defensive, and she glared at Sam.

Sam's lips tightened, and her features plainly reflected her disapproval. "Not right now, maybe, but he will be," she muttered.

CHAPTER EIGHT

The ball game was over and the Owls scored another victory. Lyn gave a prayer of thanksgiving. That should put Sam in a good mood. The girl had been quiet all week, and Lyn knew Sam was upset about her date with Burne. At first Lyn was tempted to call and tell him she had changed her mind, but she could not bring herself to do it. She decided it was best not to talk about the situation unless Sam brought up the subject. She did not.

They arrived at Ramiro's Pizza, ordered and Lyn joined Janet and Mary Ann at their table. The conversation centered on the ball game and the Owls standing in the playoffs.

"They're definitely going to make it. Today's win moves them up to second place." Janet was watching Lyn, who seemed preoccupied.

"Yes, I think so, too." Mary Ann agreed. "By the way, Lyn, will you be driving to San Antonio next Saturday?"

"Oh . . ah . . yes," Lyn answered, startled out of her reverie. "The return game with the Lady Lone Stars might be the deciding factor."

After several more minutes during which rides were arranged, Mary Ann collected her daughter and left.

"Now, Lyn DeVinney, what is going on? And don't tell me it's nothing. I know better!"

Lyn hesitated. She did not want to confide in Janet, but if she did not tell somebody she was going to burst. There was no reason to hide the blossoming relationship with Burne, but Janet was the only person she trusted not to spread it around. Her family and friends would have a field day when they found out.

Her voice neutral, Lyn replied, "I'm going out to dinner tonight with Burne MacKenzie."

Janet's brown eyes grew round and her mouth gaped. She was silent for a minute, then a smile spread slowly across her face. She reached across the table and covered Lyn's hand with her own. "You don't know how glad I am to hear that, Lyn. It's way past the time when you should be thinking of a life for yourself."

"I don't know, Janet," Lyn chewed her lip, a frown marring her features. "Sam's not too pleased about it."

"Of course not." Janet leaned forward, her expression determined. "She's had you all to herself, and it's difficult for her to accept another person changing all that. Don't worry. She'll be fine."

"I'm not sure it will be that much of a change. After all, I'm just going out to dinner with him. He may be so bored he'll never ask me out again," Lyn forced a light note into her voice.

"I doubt that." Janet replied. "Where are you going?"

"I don't know. I told him to pick the place. After all, you never know how much money a man can afford to spend."

"I wouldn't worry about that. The kind of job he has probably pays big bucks. Besides, I'm sure he has an expense account," Janet teased.

Lyn, her tone serious, responded, "I don't think Burne would do that."

Janet shook her head. "What are you going to wear?"

With a sigh, Lyn leaned back in her chair. "I've been thinking about that all week," she confessed.

"Well since you don't know where he's taking you, that makes it more difficult," Janet paused, pursing her lips. "How about that two-piece blue dress? You know, the one with the long fringed skirt. That would fit in any place."

"That's what I was thinking. I don't really have that many dressy things."

"By the way, do you need a sitter?" Janet asked. "You know Cathy would love to have Sam stay over," she grinned, a mischievous gleam in her eye.

Lyn glared, pretending to be offended. "No thanks. Lisa Gruen is going to sit with Sam."

The hands on the dainty porcelain clock on her dresser were moving much too quickly. Lyn surveyed her reflection in the mirrored closet doors. The blue dress deepened the color of her eyes to a sapphire hue and contrasted vividly with her honey blond hair. The boat-shaped neckline revealed only the tips of her collarbones while the cap sleeves bared her arms. The top part of the dress fell a scant two inches below the waistband of the full skirt which touched her calves then was fringed to just above her ankles.

A strand of pearls and pearl studs gave the ensemble an elegant look. Lyn slipped on a pair of navy blue sandals with two-inch heels and located her navy clutch bag. She nodded. Yes, it was a good choice. If she could just settle the butterflies in her stomach, she might have an enjoyable evening.

Hands clasped tightly in her lap, Lyn replayed the scene in her mind as Burne pulled onto the interstate. Lisa had arrived shortly before seven and was settling in with Sam when Burne rang the doorbell.

His eyes widened and he drew in his breath. He swallowed hard and, his voice husky, said, "You look beautiful."

Taking his eyes off the road for a minute, Burne glanced at her and grinned. "Relax, Lyn. I'm not the Big Bad Wolf about to devour Little Red Riding Hood."

In spite of herself, Lyn giggled. "Is it that obvious?"

"Only to me and I won't tell a soul."

"Thank you, sir." She settled back in her seat.

"You're welcome. Now, wouldn't you like to know where we're having dinner?"

"I admit to being a wee bit curious."

"I made reservations at the Old San Francisco Steak House. I confess I was influenced by Andy. He's the project engineer with Williams Bohrn," Burne explained. "He took his wife there the other night and couldn't stop raving about it. I hope that's all right."

"Yes, that's fine. I haven't been there for a long time, but they used to have the best steaks in town."

"Still do, according to Andy. Of course, I don't know how much attention he paid to the food. He was quite impressed with The Girl in the Red Velvet Swing."

"Naturally," Lyn replied dryly.

Burne laughed. "I'll reserve judgment until later."

Lyn sneaked a look as he concentrated on his driving. They were nearing the city and traffic was heavy. He was certainly a good-looking man. His navy blue suit fit to perfection, and the snowy white shirt and navy and red tie emphasized his gray eyes and tanned complexion.

They arrived at the restaurant and were seated quickly. The waiter appeared and Lyn chose white wine. Burne ordered Scotch and water. Silence descended once the waiter was gone. Burne looked directly into her eyes. A slow flush crept up her neck and colored her cheeks a delicate pink. She watched his eyes darken to smoky gray, and the tension in her body curled into a tight knot in her stomach. She dropped her eyes and pretended to study the menu.

Burne's voice was strained when he said, "There seems to be quite a selection on the menu. Would you like a steak or would you prefer something else?"

"Even though I know I should, I can't pass up a steak," Lyn replied, a hint of laughter in her voice.

"Why shouldn't you have steak? You certainly don't have to watch your…weight."

She ignored his reference to her figure but couldn't meet his eyes when she replied, "I'm a dietitian, remember? Red meat is not a good choice."

Burne touched her hand, which still held the menu. "Don't you think there's always a time for exceptions?" Her skin was soft beneath his fingertips. He felt her body stiffen and gently broke the contact.

"Yes." Her voice was barely above a whisper.

Before the moment grew awkward, the waiter served their drinks.

"Your waiter will be with you shortly to take your order," he told them.

They had barely touched their drinks when a waiter appeared with a huge block of cheese and a basket containing a small loaf of bread and assorted crackers. Lyn was grateful for something to occupy her hands and cut several slices of cheese and bread while Burne ordered.

Although Lyn enjoyed the perfectly cooked steak, it was difficult to keep up her end of the conversation. Burne seemed completely at ease as he made casual conversation. She realized he had lots of experience with women. Why, most men his age were married and had families. Her thoughts flew to Sam. It was the first time she had given a thought to her daughter.

Burne caught the surprised look on her face. "Is something wrong?"

"Oh, no. I was just wondering how Sam and Lisa are getting along." She concentrated on cutting a bite of steak.

Burne's smile was meant to be reassuring. "I'm sure they're doing fine."

"Yes, I am too. But this is the first time Sam has stayed with anyone other than Janet or family."

"You mean she's never had a sitter before?" he asked, amazement showing plainly on his face.

"Not in the true sense of the word. It's never been necessary." Lyn was immediately on the defensive.

Burne shook his head. "You are a most unusual mother, but then, Sam is an unusual little girl."

Lyn's eyes narrowed, and she stared at him. "Why do you say that?" Her voice was tinged with frost.

Burne cursed under his breath. "I'm sorry. I didn't mean to sound critical. Quite the contrary. It was meant as a compliment. You seem to be doing an excellent job as a single parent."

Lyn continued to stare at him. He probably knew Sam was illegitimate since it was common knowledge at The Manor. *Does he think because I succumbed once that I have no morals; that I will fall victim to his charm that easily?*

Burne watched the changing expressions flit across Lyn's face and the rejection in her eyes. "I mean it, Lyn. I do admire you."

Her thoughts whirling round and round, Lyn took a deep breath. Suddenly, she wanted desperately to believe him. She had never been overly concerned what others thought as long as she was doing what she believed was right for Sam. For some reason she wouldn't admit, it was important that he respect her.

"Thank you."

Burne heaved a sigh of relief. The waiter approached and they declined dessert. He ordered coffee.

"When is the next ball game? Dad really enjoys them."

"It's here in San Antonio next Saturday. Speaking of your father, he seems more content now that the Schumanns are back." She smoothed the napkin in her lap.

"Yes, I think he is. Myra and Joe spend a lot of time with him, and I'm grateful. Especially since things are getting a bit complicated at the job site, and I don't have as much free time."

"I suppose a big project like that has quite a few problems."

"Yes," he admitted, "of one kind or another."

The highlight of the evening arrived. The Girl in the Red Velvet Swing spoke to the crowd and took her place in the contraption built high above the bar. She was clad in a skimpy red costume that revealed a curvaceous figure and a pair of shapely legs in black stockings and high-heeled red pumps. The crowd quieted down while they watched her daring performance as she swung high in the air. Lyn covertly observed Burne as the girl went through her act, but she found his eyes on her instead. He caught her watching him, winked mischievously and turned toward the show. She thought she heard him say, "You're much prettier," but she couldn't be sure because the crowd erupted into loud applause.

The entertainment over and their coffee finished, there was no reason to linger. Burne called for the check, left a generous tip and escorted Lyn from the restaurant.

"I'm not that familiar with the popular night spots, but I'd be happy to take you someplace for an after-dinner drink." He unlocked the Suburban and opened the door.

"Thank you, but I should really be getting home. I don't want to keep Lisa up too late."

Burne nodded. "I understand."

As they sped up I-10, Lyn broke the silence. "I want to thank you for a lovely dinner, Burne. I enjoyed it very much." She knew she sounded stiff and formal, but she did not know what else to say.

"You're welcome, Lyn. It was my pleasure. I hope you enjoyed it enough to go out with me again."

She *had* enjoyed being with him and wondered if she dared risk another evening in his company. His was a temporary situation and could not lead to anything serious. Not that she was interested in a serious relationship, but...

"It might be arranged," she teased and did not know where her answer came from. Her emotions were interfering with her common sense, and she could not seem to control either one.

Burne grinned as he glanced at her out of the corner of his eye. "I have an idea, but I'm not sure you'll go along with it."

She turned her head and looked at him. "You won't know unless you tell me about it." A tiny smile hovered around her mouth.

"Well, you said Sam will be playing a game in San Antonio Saturday morning. Why don't the two of you plan to spend the day with me? We could take in the Riverwalk, the Alamo, that sort of thing."

"I don't know about that. Sam is always a mess after she plays. She wouldn't be presentable, I'm afraid." Lyn knew Sam would object, and she needed time to organize her argument.

"No problem. She can clean up at my place."

His place? Burne met her gaze for a second, and she knew her reaction amused him.

"Don't you think you would be properly chaperoned?"

"It's not that. I just don't know how Sam would react to it." She would not insult his intelligence by offering some kind of flimsy excuse.

"The worst that can happen is that she will refuse. What do you say?"

Lyn mulled it over in her mind for a second. "All right. I'll ask her."

They reached the exit to Mt. Laurel, and Burne slowed for the ramp. The evening had only deepened his interest in her. He ached to hold her in his arms and kiss her, but he knew he would scare her off if he tried. He had to take it slowly even though it was becoming more difficult each time he saw her. He had not been intimate with a woman for quite some time, but Lyn was more than just someone to hop into bed with. She was special if he could only convince her that his intentions were honorable. Honorable intentions? He barely knew her, but that did not seem to make any difference in the way he felt.

He pulled into a parking space and cut the ignition. His thoughts were racing. What should he do? He couldn't very well shake her hand and bid her good night. They reached her door all too soon.

"I would ask you in Burne, but I have to see Lisa home." Lyn told him, grateful she didn't have to invent an excuse.

"Does she live far?"

"No. She lives in the complex." She fished her keys from her purse and looked up at him. "Thank you again for a lovely evening," her voice was low and soft.

Taking her key, he inserted it in the lock then turned to face her. "I'm glad you had a good time. I know I did." He took her hands in his and kissed her fingertips. He felt her stiffen but she didn't pull away. Gently releasing her, he stepped back. "I'll call you next week. Good night, Lyn."

She swallowed, took a deep breath, exhaled slowly and managed to find her voice. "Good night, Burne."

Lisa reported that Sam had finished her homework, and they had watched television before Sam went to bed. Everything had gone well although Lisa thought Sam was much too quiet. Lyn knew the child was trying to come to terms with her mother's interest in Burne. How would she react when Lyn told her about his invitation for Saturday?

Sleep was a long time coming. Lyn's mind went over the evening with Burne. A vision of his silver eyes and heart-stopping grin danced behind her closed eyelids. When he kissed her fingertips a shiver ran down her spine, and it had nothing to do with being cold. For the first time since Kevin, she had enjoyed a man's touch. She admitted she was attracted to Burne and wanted to see him again. His interest in her was obvious, but what about Sam? Did he really want to spend time with both of them? He was smart enough to know that she would never neglect her daughter or force her into a relationship.

She tossed about, trying to put Burne from her mind. Was he having difficulty getting to sleep? She imagined him stretched out full length in bed. Unbidden images of his chest, bare and muscled, perhaps covered with fine sandy hair, popped into her head. Her body felt warm and her gown was suddenly too tight. No! She refused to let her imagination carry the illusion any farther. She punched her pillow, grateful that tomorrow was not a workday.

CHAPTER NINE

Burne and Andy were alone in the office. It had been a frustrating day. Two SAPD detectives had shown up early that morning and talked with just about everybody at the job site.

"Do you think they picked up any clues?" Andy asked.

"I don't know. It's hard to tell about those guys. They don't give anything away," Burne replied.

"The one named Brandenburg spent quite awhile with Carlos Romero." Andy leaned back in his chair.

"Carlos is more familiar with what's in stock than any of the others. He probably checks in more material than Dan does. He's a big help with the inventory count, too." Finishing the notes he was making, Burne swiveled his chair to face Andy.

"I noticed the other one, Delgado, talking with Pete Martinez. They seemed pretty friendly," Andy remarked.

"I'm sure Pete has been on other jobs where material turned up missing. You know, it's happened on more than a few of ours," Burne reminded him.

"Yeah. Comes with the territory, I guess." Andy stood up and stretched. "It's time for me to head on home. Shelley will have dinner waiting. Good night."

"Give Amy a big hug for me."

"Will do. And by the way, Shelley wants you to come to dinner one night next week. You can even bring a date." A grin spread across Andy's face.

"I just might do that," Burne teased.

Andy's grin vanished and he scrutinized Burne's face. "Are you serious? Have you met someone?"

"Maybe. But it's too soon to fill you in."

"Come on, now. This is old Andy you're talking to," he coaxed.

"Go home Andy. Shelley will be worried." Burne regretted having referred to Lyn, and he had no intention of giving Andy any more information.

The tone of his voice or the look on his face must have discouraged Andy, because he dropped the subject and left the office without further comment.

Burne switched off the computer and tidied up his desk. He was going to the health club for a swim and wondered if Paul Mansfield would be there. He had not seen the chef since their initial meeting at the pool. Had Lyn told Paul about their dinner date? He doubted it. Lyn was too reserved to share her private life with her employees.

A vision of her vivid blue eyes flashed before him. He could almost feel her soft skin when he had held her hand across the table. Would the rest of her body be as silky smooth? She was slender, but he could tell she had curves in all the right places. His body responded in typical male fashion. *Damn!* A few laps in the pool should cool him off.

* * *

"Mom, I don't want to do it!" Sam howled.

"You know I won't force you, Sam."

Dinner was over and they were sitting at the table discussing Saturday's trip to San Antonio. When Lyn told Sam about Burne's suggestion, she was horrified. There was no way she wanted to shower and dress in a strange man's apartment and, as far as she was concerned, Burne was a stranger.

Seeing the satisfied smirk on Sam's face, Lyn's temper flared. She bit back the angry words she wanted to say. The realization had been slow in coming, but she finally admitted she might have given Sam too much of herself. For the first time since the child was born, Lyn wanted to put herself first. She was not going to deny she enjoyed Burne's company and the attention he was paying her. Her daughter's well-being was the most important thing in the world, but there had to be a way to overcome Sam's objections without giving in to her.

"All right, young lady. You don't have to clean up at Burne's apartment, but we're going to spend the afternoon with him. I'm sure he won't mind a *grungy* little girl tagging along." Lyn rose and started clearing the table.

"Mom, you don't mean it! You know I can't go any place looking that way," she pleaded, her lips forming a classic pout.

"I don't see any alternative, do you?" Lyn answered bluntly.

Lyn's heartbeat accelerated as she recognized the voice on the other end of the line. She was expecting Burne's call, but his voice did things to her emotions.

"Are we on for Saturday?"

"I think so, but..." Lyn hesitated. She was embarrassed to tell him about Sam's refusal to go to his apartment.

"But what?"

"We may be accompanied by a girl in a dirty baseball uniform." There, it was out.

Burne's laughter erupted in her ear. "Is that all? You had me worried. I thought you were going to back out."

"No. Sam isn't going to get her way this time. She is usually very conscious of her appearance, and I'm sure she'll change her mind." Lyn toyed with the pen in her hand.

"It won't matter to me if she doesn't as long as you spend the afternoon with me."

They decided on travel arrangements. Lyn and Sam would ride to the ballpark with Janet or Mary Ann. Burne would meet them there and drive them home later. Lyn realized that once she made their plans known, the relationship would be out in the open. She gave a sigh of relief. She had nothing to hide.

* * *

The Owls were defeated by the Lady Lone Stars again, and their loss served to deepen Sam's ugly mood. She was clinging to her refusal to go to Burne's apartment, and Lyn had not bothered with a change of clothing. Her own khaki slacks and colorful camp shirt worn with white athletic shoes were suitable for the day's activities. Burne showed up at the ballpark a few minutes before the game started wearing jeans and a yellow knit shirt.

Lyn mentally cringed thinking about Sam's appearance. Could she really go through with her plan and let Sam accompany them in her dirty uniform? She watched Burne out of the corner of her eye. Would the embarrassment be worth it? Somehow she did not think it would bother him, and she was not going to cancel their date. *I hope this doesn't make matters worse between them.*

The crowd was dispersing and Lyn and Burne reached the Owls just as Sam walked away from her teammates. True to form, her uniform was dusty and her face was streaked with dirt. Lyn swallowed and her resolve wavered. She fished in her purse for a handful of tissues and handed them to Sam. "Use these and see if you can clean your face and hands."

Sam's eyes narrowed and she glared at her mother. "You don't want me to go looking like this, do you?"

"We discussed this Sam, and I thought I made myself clear. Now clean up your face." Her voice brooked no argument.

Burne pretended to be watching the crowd.

"I'm sorry Burne. I know this is embarrassing for you, but I can't give in to her. I did bring her an extra pair of shoes," she indicated the plastic bag she was carrying.

Burne reached for her hand, and clasp it gently. "Don't worry about it. I'm not the least bit embarrassed. Try to relax. Everything is going to be all right."

She gave him a weak smile. "I hope so."

His eyes were filled with concern, and her pulse began to beat rapidly. As they stared into each other's eyes, the sounds around them faded away, and they were suspended in time. Lyn's eyes opened wide, and she watched as his pupils dilate and the silver darkened to pewter. Hesitantly his free hand touched the top of her head and slid down to the nape of her neck. She stood perfectly still, her gaze locked on his.

"Lyn." His voice was husky.

She knew he was going to kiss her, and she was powerless to stop him. The bright sunshine, the remnants of the crowd, the sounds of motors being started, all the activity of a normal Saturday morning at the ballpark vanished. Rational thought disappeared in the magic that surrounded them. Fear, apprehension, propriety, all faded away as Lyn watched Burne's head lower while his hand held hers in a firm grip. His lips were mere inches away when an indignant voice penetrated their dream world.

"Mom! I can't get the dirt off without soap."

Lyn jumped, her face turning a fiery red while Burne released his hold on her and took a step backward. Tearing her eyes away, she looked up to see Sam approaching. She was scrubbing at her face with the tissues while her baseball cleats churned up tiny dust devils around her feet. Realization hit Lyn like a bolt of lightning. What was she doing? She would have allowed Burne to kiss her in broad daylight, in plain sight of the people lingering on the field, in the parking lot and, worse yet, her daughter. Waves of shame washed over her, and she could not look at Burne or Sam.

Taking a deep breath and exhaling slowly, Lyn took the tissues from Sam. "Let me see what I can do." Her voice sounded faint to her own ears. She scrubbed at the dirt on Sam's face and hoped the girl did not notice her hands were trembling.

"That's the best I can do. Wipe your hands then throw these in the trashcan."

The ballpark was almost deserted as they walked to the parking lot. When they were settled in the Suburban, Burne suggested lunch. "Would you like to eat now or wait until we get to the Riverwalk?"

Neither Lyn nor Sam answered immediately. Sam's appearance was still a sore spot with her, and she knew the girl fully expected her to beg off for the afternoon. "What would you like to do?" she asked Burne.

"It doesn't matter to me. You choose the place."

If she was going to stick to her decision, it should be the Riverwalk. There were dozens of places to eat and, in order to save a remnant of Sam's pride, she would choose a restaurant that offered outside dining. Turning to Burne, she asked, "Do you like Mexican food?"

He grinned, pleased with her choice. "It's one of my favorites."

Descending the steps to the Riverwalk, Burne marveled at the engineering feat that had created the sub-tropical paradise. Trees, shrubs and plants native to the area provided an unending canopy of shade for the winding walk ways. Hundreds of blooming flowers added a blaze of color among the various shades of green. People of all ages, sizes and ethnic backgrounds mingled on the sidewalks while the barges bore sightseers through the long maze of waterways.

This was not Burne's first trip to the Riverwalk and Lyn and Sam had grown up with it, but the festive mood of the crowd was infectious. Lyn gave Sam the extra pair of shoes, which served to eliminate some of her hostility.

Choosing Garcia's, they were served steaming platters of enchiladas, refried beans and Spanish rice with side dishes of guacamole. Burne ordered beer while Lyn and Sam chose iced tea. The conversation was strained at first until the antics of the birds looking for tidbits broke the ice. They flitted around, their bright eyes capable of finding the tiniest crumb.

"Look, Mom! That white pigeon and one of the grackles are trying to pick up the same piece of food." Sam pointed to the birds that were warily approaching the morsel.

The large shiny black bird with a long split tail, strutted up to the plump bird, its golden eyes fixed on the food. The pigeon cooed softly and, true to nature, graciously left the tidbit to the more aggressive hunter.

"That's not fair," Sam complained. Her sympathies were plainly with the pigeon.

"No, I suppose not, but it's the way life is, Sam. There will always be strong people taking things away from the weaker ones."

Burne detected the note of sadness that Lyn tried to disguise. "Perhaps it's plain old-fashioned courtesy that's missing. Pigeons are noted for being gentle, you know. Now, how about dessert?" he tempted.

"Ice cream," Sam announced.

Burne was amused to see Sam's bad mood had not affected her appetite. He chose flan and Lyn ordered lemon ice. Feeling stuffed and reasonably content, all agreed that a visit to the Alamo was in order. Burne took care of the check, and they climbed the steps to the street.

The hallowed atmosphere, in spite of the crowd, was filled with feelings of humility and admiration. Called *The Cradle of Texas Liberty*, the shrine dedicated to those whose lives were sacrificed for Texas freedom, brought a lump to the throat of the most hardened visitor. The shady grounds, cooled by giant live oaks and mesquite trees, provided ample opportunity for a leisurely stroll. Sam raced away to explore the buildings that were once occupied by the priests and workers at the mission.

"Burne, I want to thank you for today. It has been good for Sam and for me." It was difficult to explain what she meant. Burne's easy acceptance of Sam's rebellion, his lack of concern about her appearance was all mixed up with her feelings.

Burne motioned to a stone bench beside the pathway. When she was seated, he did not sit down but stood facing her with one foot propped up on the bench.

"I think I understand what you're trying to say, Lyn, but you don't need to thank me. I'm just glad you decided to spend the day with me. I hope you're willing to let me take you and Sam out again. She's a good kid, so don't be too hard on her."

In spite of her uncertainty, Lyn smiled. "It's nice to know we haven't turned you off."

Burne's foot came down off the bench; he straightened to his full height and looked down at her. "Turn me off? Believe me lady, you have nothing to worry about," he replied dryly.

Lyn dropped her eyes. She didn't know what to say nor could she have spoken if she had found the words. Sam chose that moment to join them, and the spell was broken.

"I like to come here. It's neat," the girl enthused as she plopped down beside Lyn.

"I think it's time we started home," Lyn suggested.

"Ah, Mom, do we have to?" Sam begged.

"Yes. It takes awhile to get to Mt. Laurel, and Burne is probably tired. I know I am." She confessed, getting to her feet.

The tone of her voice, the slump of her shoulders, the look in her eyes told Burne not to argue with her decision. Instead, he merely replied, "We can leave any time you're ready."

Burne picked up I-10 and they drove north toward Mt. Laurel. Lyn was quiet and, when Burne glanced in the rear view mirror, he saw that Sam had fallen asleep.

"She's had a hard day," he remarked as he pointed toward the back seat.

"Oh?" She turned and saw Sam sprawled out on her side, her mouth slightly open and breathing deeply. Lyn smiled and spoke softly. "Yes, but I'm sure she had a good time."

"I think so, too. She's a fine girl, Lyn."

"Thank you." Lyn was silent for a minute. "I'm sure you're aware of Sam's background. I've made no secret of it."

"I don't pay much attention to gossip."

Lyn glanced over her shoulder to confirm that Sam was still sleeping. Her voice barely above a whisper, she continued. "You know, I've never had a...a relationship with a man since...since Sam was born."

"It doesn't matter, Lyn. All I'm concerned with is *now*, and how you feel about *me*."

"I think that should be obvious," she laughed softly.

Glancing out of the corner of his eye, he grinned and replied, "I hope so."

They lapsed into a comfortable silence. All too soon they reached the apartment complex.

"Are we home already?" Sam sat up and rubbed her eyes.

"Yes, sleepy head, we're home," Lyn teased. Turning to Burne she asked, "Would you like to come up for something cold to drink?"

Burne was sorely tempted, but his instincts told him to give Lyn time and space. "No, thanks. I'll take a rain check, though. I thought I would go past The Manor and say hello to Dad."

"I'm sure he would appreciate that. And Burne, thank you again for a lovely day. We enjoyed it very much." Lyn looked pointedly at her daughter.

Sam, looking sheepish, dropped her eyes and muttered, "Yeah, I had fun. Thank you...Burne."

"You're both very welcome. I had a good time too. Lyn, I'll call you next week. Okay?"

She nodded. They were standing in the parking lot, in broad daylight, with her daughter observing every movement. "Please do. And thank you again."

Burne grinned and Lyn's heart did a flip flop in her chest. He hopped into the Suburban, waved and drove off.

Texas Enchiladas

Serves 4 to 6

1 pound ground beef
Salt and pepper to taste
1 teaspoon garlic powder
1 teaspoon ground cumin
3 tablespoons chili powder
2 tablespoons cornstarch
1 ½ quarts water or beef broth
1 package (12) corn tortillas
vegetable oil

1 pound cheddar cheese (may use more
if desired)
1 medium onion, chopped

For sauce, in large saucepan or Dutch oven, brown ground beef with garlic powder, salt, and pepper. Drain. Add water or broth, chili powder, and cumin. Mix well. Bring to a boil. Reduce heat and simmer uncovered for 1/2 hour. In small bowl, mix cornstarch and small amount of cold water until cornstarch is completely dissolved. Gradually add to chili sauce stirring constantly. Continue cooking 5 minutes.

For enchiladas, heat oven 350 degrees. Heat about ½ inch oil in small skillet until hot but not smoking. Quickly fry each tortilla in oil to soften, about 2 seconds on each side. Drain on paper towels. Combine cheese and onion. Spoon about 1/3 cup cheese mixture down center of each tortilla. Roll up and place seam side down in baking pan. Top with chili sauce. Cover with foil. Bake 10 minutes or until hot. Remove foil. Sprinkle more cheese on top. Continue baking 2 minutes or until cheese melts.

Spanish Rice

Serves 6

3 tablespoons cooking oil
2 cups uncooked rice
¼ cup chopped bell pepper
¼ cup chopped onion
5 cups water
1 tomato, chopped
1 teaspoon salt
2 large cloves garlic, pressed
1 teaspoon cumin seed, crushed
2 or 3 peppercorns, ground

In a heavy pot, slowly fry rice, pepper and onions until yellow. Add water, tomato and spices. Bring to a boil. Reduce heat. Cover and simmer until rice is tender and liquid is absorbed, approximately 25 minutes.

CHAPTER TEN

"Was there something else, Paul?" Lyn paused from gathering up the files on the conference room table.

Paul lingered after Theresa and Gertrude returned to their duties. "I was just wondering… It's really none of my business," he stammered.

"What's none of your business?" Lyn asked, smiling.

"Well, I may as well go ahead and stick my nose where it doesn't belong. There's talk going around the kitchen that you're dating Burne MacKenzie."

Turning to face Paul she questioned, "Why would that be of interest to anyone?"

A dull flush suffused Paul's tanned features. "I guess it's because we didn't think you were interested in men."

After a minute of strained silence, Lyn replied, "As you said, it really is a personal matter." Turning away, she walked into the hallway.

"I'm sorry, Lyn. I wish…" his voice trailed off.

Glancing around to assure herself they were alone, she asked, "You wish what? Let's clear the air."

"If I had known you would consider it, I would have asked you out myself."

Shocked, Lyn stared at him. She had never had a romantic thought about Paul. She liked and depended on him, but there could never be anything between them even if Burne MacKenzie had not come into her life.

"I know I'm not putting this very well. I value your friendship, but it's never wise to become involved when both parties work together." How well she could testify to that piece of advice!

"I suppose you're right." Paul's tone rang hollow.

"I'm flattered, really I am. But you should concentrate on someone your age. There are a lot of pretty girls in this area."

"Yeah, I noticed." There was no humor in his smile.

"I'm sure you have." Lyn forced a light laugh.

As they reached the hall that led to the dining services wing, Myra got off the elevator. She greeted them warmly. "Hello, there!"

They barely acknowledged her greeting before she rushed on. "Lyn, I've been wanting to talk with you. Do you have a minute?"

"Of course. I'm on my way back to my office."

Paul muttered something Lyn didn't catch and continued on to the kitchen.

Entering her office, Lyn motioned Myra toward a chair. The woman seemed flustered as she smoothed her blue chambray skirt with quick movements. She avoided looking directly at Lyn. "I don't want you to think I'm a busybody that repeats gossip, but I couldn't help hearing that you and Burne are seeing one another."

Lyn gasped. Twice in less than fifteen minutes she was hearing her private life discussed. Irritation, embarrassment, indignation, all warred for first place in her emotions.

Her distress must have been reflected in her face, because Myra hastened to add, "Oh, my dear, please forgive me. It really is none of my business, but Bessie was all excited about it when she came to clean yesterday."

Bessie was one of the maids on the housekeeping staff.

"What did Bessie tell you, Mrs. Schumann?"

"Oh, my! I don't want to get Bessie into trouble. I like her and she does a good job." Myra fidgeted with her earring.

"I'm sure she does." Lyn kept her voice neutral.

"She knows that the MacKenzies are old friends of ours, and I guess she didn't see any harm in mentioning it to me."

Lyn's face colored a bright red, but she managed to hold back the sharp retort that hovered on the edge of her tongue. After a minute she responded, "I don't understand why everybody is so interested in my social life." Her tone was civil but cool.

Myra squirmed in her seat. "Please don't take offense, dear. I'm just glad it's Burne. I've known him most of his life, and he's a fine young man."

Lyn smiled in spite of herself. "I think so too, Mrs. Schumann, but don't put too much emphasis on our...friendship. We've only known each other a short time."

"I know Burne, and he won't continue seeing you if he isn't serious. There was a girl when he was in college, but they broke up when he went into the Air Force."

"I wondered if he had ever been married," Lyn commented.

"No, he hasn't." Myra smiled and visibly relaxed in her chair.

"We don't really know much about each other. He's included Sam in our dates, and there hasn't been much opportunity to talk about ourselves." Her mood lifted and she returned Myra's smile.

With a sigh Myra stood up. "Now that I've made a complete fool of myself, I'd better let you get back to your work."

"I'm not at all offended Mrs. Schumann, just a little embarrassed to be the object of so much gossip. But I'm really glad to learn more about Burne. Not that I had any doubts about his character," she hastened to add, getting to her feet.

"Then I'm forgiven for being an interfering old woman?" she asked with a smile.

"There's nothing to forgive," Lyn assured her.

"I think you're just right for him, Lyn. But I promise not to try match-making." The glint in her blue eyes belied the truth of her words.

* * *

A million bright stars twinkled in the midnight blue sky. Burne stopped outside the office door and took a deep breath of fresh air. Although air conditioning was a godsend, he enjoyed being outdoors. He flexed his shoulders and stretched his neck. Working on the computer most of the day his arms ached, and there was a dull pain between his shoulder blades. Andy had left long ago, but Burne skipped dinner and finished up. A swim in the club pool sounded great, but he knew it would be closed this time of night.

Burne, debating whether to stop for something to eat, saw a dark form move in the vicinity of the tool sheds. He stepped out of the light and stood watching as the figure disappeared. Was it the security guard or could it be somebody connected with the missing materials?

"You're here kinda late, aren't you Mr. MacKenzie?" The deep voice came from the opposite direction.

Burne turned as Tom Schneider came into view. He calculated the distance between the office and the tool sheds. There was no way Tom could have been the figure he saw moving in the shadows. He walked toward the guard with his finger to his lips.

Tom darted quick glances around then, his voice barely above a whisper, asked, "What's up?"

"Over by the tool sheds. It was just a shadow but it moved."

"Stay put!" Tom drew his revolver and ran on silent feet toward the sheds.

Ignoring the guard's command, Burne followed him. As Tom disappeared into the darkness, Burne reached the first shed and halted. He fumbled with the locks on the tool-shed door. They were intact. The second shed was only a few feet away. He reached it in a matter of seconds. Searching in the darkness, he found the locks. One of them was secured, but the other was dangling. Evidently the thief had been interrupted before he could get the door open.

A beam of light shone full in Burne's face, and Tom exclaimed, "Mr. MacKenzie, you shouldn't be here. It's too dangerous."

Burne exhaled the breath he had been holding and gave a sigh of relief. "I guess I didn't think about it. Look, one of these locks has been pried open."

The guard fixed his light on the shed door and came forward. "Did you touch it?"

"Yeah," Burne answered with a sheepish grin.

Tom shook his head. "The boys will want to dust it anyway. Wait a minute—I don't think it's been pried open. Looks more like it was opened with a key. Maybe your men forgot to lock it before they left."

Burne's eyes narrowed thoughtfully. "Maybe. Or maybe somebody has a set of keys."

"Could be," Tom nodded. "I need to call this in and get a couple of guys out here." He headed for the lighted office.

An hour later, the excitement over, Burne locked the office door and bid Tom good night. He no longer felt like eating and drove straight home. A steaming hot shower followed by a stinging cold rinse revived his flagging energy. He reviewed the night's events, and the result of the police investigation. After a thorough search in which nothing out of the ordinary was discovered, the police decided a would-be burglar had been scared off. They confiscated the lock for fingerprints, but the likelihood was small there would be any.

Stretched out on the bed, wearing only a pair of white cotton briefs, Burne knew sleep was going to be a long time coming. His mind fastened on the bottle of Scotch in the kitchen cabinet. Climbing out of bed, he padded barefoot through the living room. He poured a tumbler half full of liquor and filled it with ice.

Returning to the bedroom, he sat on the edge of the bed and downed a healthy swallow. It slid down his throat, as smooth as silk, and brought with it the sensation of satin-smooth skin beneath his fingertips. *Ah, Lyn.* He had intended to call her tonight. Glancing at the clock on the nightstand, he saw it was after midnight. *Too late!*

The liquor hit his stomach like a blow to the gut. He finished the remainder while thoughts of Lyn and Sam tumbled around in his head. He was becoming disoriented and sleepy. Three or four shots of Scotch on an empty stomach. *Christ!* Even a green kid knew better. His last conscious thought was to call Lyn first thing in the morning.

* * *

The phone rang as Lyn picked up her purse and car keys. *Now, who could that be so early in the morning?* Hiding her agitation, she answered. "Hello, Lyn."

Burne's voice was husky as if he had just gotten out of bed. "I'm sorry to call you so early, but I've been tied up at work, and it was too late when I got home. I wanted to ask you out tomorrow night, if you're not busy."

Lyn's heart fluttered, then raced on causing her breath to catch in her throat. Burne hadn't called since their outing at the Riverwalk, and she was sure he had lost interest after Sam's display of poor manners.

"Lyn?" he repeated.

"I'm sorry. You surprised me. I was just leaving for work."

"Would you rather I call you later?"

"No, it's all right. Thank you for asking me out, but I have plans for tomorrow evening."

"I see," he told her, his voice curt.

Lyn felt a small flicker of satisfaction. "I don't know what you 'see,' but I'm going to a dietetic association meeting."

"Where is this meeting and what time does it start?"

"It's at the health science center, and it starts at 7:30. Why? Are you checking up on me?" she teased.

"As a matter of fact, I am."

Lyn gasped. "Are you serious?"

"If you mean am I serious about you, the answer is 'yes.' Am I serious about checking up on you, in a way. I thought maybe we could have an early dinner. We'll both be in the same vicinity. You could still get to your meeting on time."

"I usually fix Sam a snack, then drop her off at Janet's. Let me see if I can make some different arrangements. Would it be all right if I called you at your office?"

"Sure." He gave her the number.

"I have to go Burne or Sam will be late for school. I'll call you as soon as possible."

Lyn didn't want to discuss Burne with Janet. The relationship was too new, too fragile. She would ask Lisa to spend the evening with Sam.

Lyn had no sooner arrived at The Manor when Standsbury knocked on her door, his expression grim.

Lyn stood and pushed back her chair. "Good morning, Dean. Please come in."

He walked into the room and closed the door behind him.

"I'm afraid I have some disturbing news, Lyn. Lawrence MacKenzie became ill during the night and rang for help. Peggy Canova was on duty, and when she responded he complained of nausea and diarrhea and said the fish he had for dinner was spoiled. He wasn't running a fever, but Peggy called his doctor who prescribed treatment. She kept a close watch on him all night, and he seems to be recovering." Standsbury sunk down in one of the chairs before Lyn's desk.

Lyn's eyes widened and she gaped at him. "Has anyone else taken ill?"

He shook his head. "Not that we know about. That's what's so puzzling about it. If the fish was tainted, it looks like the other residents who ate it would be sick."

Lyn shook her head. "I can't believe the fish was spoiled." This was the nightmare every dietitian dreaded.

"Regardless, we have to take some kind of action. What do you suggest?"

"I'll speak with Paul right away. If there are any fish remaining in the freezer, we'll dispose of them immediately. In fact, I'd like to send a sample out to be analyzed. That way we can be sure we're protected."

"That sounds reasonable to me." Standsbury rose. "Let me know as soon as you learn anything."

"Of course."

Lyn debated if she should visit the elder MacKenzie in his apartment but decided against it. She'd wait until she got the results from the food lab. It would only take a day or two, and she would know if the fish had been spoiled. Either way she needed to arm herself, because she knew she could expect no mercy from the cantankerous old man.

"Thank you very much, Tammy. You don't know how relieved I am to hear that. Fax me the complete results as soon as they're available."

Lyn replaced the receiver and heaved a sigh of relief. She dropped her head. Thank God no contaminants had been found in the samples of the fish sent to the lab for analysis.

Lyn looked up to see Lawrence MacKenzie walking into her office hurling accusations at her.

Lyn's eyes narrowed as she fought her rising temper. Nothing would be gained by getting into a shouting match with him.

"Mr. MacKenzie, I apologize for not contacting you, but I was waiting on the lab report. It just came in by phone. The fax should be here in a day or so. No contaminants were found in the fish." Her voice was calm, but her emotions were a mass of raw nerves.

"Humph!" he muttered.

"Please sit down, sir. We need to discuss this rationally." Lyn settled in her chair, looked him in the eye and waited.

"I'll stand, if you don't mind." Lawrence stuck out his chin and, his tone belligerent, told her, "I don't care what the report says, I know the fish was bad."

"What else did you have besides the fish?" Lyn questioned.

"I had a baked potato, carrots and a tossed salad. Sure nothing there to make me sick. It was the fish!" he insisted.

"Did you have dessert?"

"Yes. I don't remember what it was called, but it was some kind of lemon pudding. Not very tasty," he complained.

He referred to a diabetic refrigerator dessert. Made with artificial sweetener and non-dairy topping, it contained nothing that would account for his illness.

"I don't believe it could have been caused by any of your other food choices. What puzzles me is that nobody else reported an illness."

MacKenzie, a sheepish look replacing his agitation, looked down at his feet. Then lifting his head, he muttered, "Maybe they didn't tell you about it."

"Oh, I'm sure it would have been reported," Lyn replied dryly.

"Maybe, maybe not." Lawrence MacKenzie rose and left without another word.

* * *

Pulling into the coffee shop parking lot, Lyn caught a glimpse of Burne. He walked toward her and she saw his welcoming smile. Her heart fluttered and her pulse raced. In olive green Dockers and a green and white striped shirt, open at the neck, he looked tanned and fit.

"I'm really glad you could make it."

"I'm afraid we don't have much time," she told him.

"What is it they say about quality versus quantity?" he teased.

The hostess seated them and the waitress took their order right away.

Lyn wondered if Lawrence had phoned Burne about his illness, but she didn't want to wait for Burne to bring it up. "Have you talked with your father in the last couple of days?" She toyed with her flatware.

"No, I've been in and out of the office a lot. Why? Is something wrong?" Burne's face took on a questioning look.

Lyn drew a deep breath, exhaled slowly and related the *fish story*.

Burne was silent for a minute, his brow furrowed in thought. "You say the lab report came back negative for contaminants?"

"Yes, absolutely. I just don't understand how he could have become ill from what he ate in the dining room." Lyn searched Burn's face for signs of accusation.

The silence grew awkward before a grin slowly appeared on his face. "Looks like Dad is up to his old tricks."

"Tricks? I don't understand."

"It sounds ridiculous, I know, but Dad used to pull that stunt at

Annie's. We finally figured out he just wanted attention." He chuckled, remembering.

"That's not funny, Burne. He caused The Manor more than a few anxious moments." Lyn's voice ended on a sharp note.

Burne's eyebrows rose, but his voice was even when he replied, "I know it isn't. Do you want me to talk with him?"

Lyn opened her mouth to respond but, seeing the look in Burne's eyes, shook her head. He wasn't responsible for his father's actions.

All too soon they were finished, and Burne walked Lyn to her car. She thanked him for dinner, but he seemed reluctant to let her go.

"Does Sam have a game Saturday?"

"No, the play-offs don't start until the following Saturday." She unlocked the car door.

"How about spending the day with me? I'm sure we could find something to do that Sam would enjoy."

Lyn was thoughtful for a moment. Burne had played host a number of times, and she should reciprocate in some way. "I have a better idea. Why don't you come to our place for dinner Saturday night? I'm really a pretty good cook," she smiled mischievously.

"I'm sure you are, and I accept. What time should I be there?"

"Is six o'clock too early?"

"No, that's fine." He opened the door for her.

"Good. Thanks for dinner. I have to leave, or I'll be late." She slid under the steering wheel.

"I understand. And thanks for the invitation. I'm looking forward to it. Good night, Lyn." He closed the door and stepped away from the car.

CHAPTER ELEVEN

Lyn waited until the following evening to tell Sam that Burne was coming to dinner on Saturday. Throughout the day the task loomed before her. She dreaded discussing it with Sam and, it would be a discussion; she had no doubt of that!

Lyn was sitting on the sofa when Sam entered the living room.

"Mom, I've finished my homework. Can I watch some TV before I take a bath?"

Ignoring Sam's lapse in grammar, Lyn motioned to the space beside her. "I have something to tell you."

"What is it, Mom? Is something wrong? Are Grandma and Grandpa all right?"

Lyn's parents lived in San Antonio, but she didn't see them often. They owned a RV and traveled a great deal.

"Everybody is fine, Sam. This has to do with Burne."

Sam was silent. Her eyes focused on her mother for a minute then her gaze wavered, and she looked down at the floor.

"Sam?" Lyn questioned. "Do you remember what I told you when you were spending a lot of time at Cathy's?"

Sam looked up, a frown on her face. "You said I should invite Cathy to come to our house."

"That's right and why did I say that?"

"Well, you said it was rude not to ask Cathy to come here since I spent so much time at her house."

"Wouldn't it be rude to accept Burne's invitations without doing something for him in return?"

"Yeah, I guess so," Sam agreed but Lyn heard the reluctance in her voice.

"That's what I've done. I invited Burne to have dinner with us Saturday night."

"The kids at the center say he's your *boyfriend*," she blurted out, shifting in her seat.

Lyn sat back and considered her answer carefully. At this point she could not honestly deny a relationship was developing but it had yet to become romantic. Why, he had never even kissed her! She knew he wanted to and a secret part of her was thrilled.

She met Sam's eyes as she replied, "No, Sam, he isn't my boyfriend. We're *friends*, that's all."

With a look far too speculative for her age, Sam nodded but made no further comment. She jumped up, TV forgotten, and started down the hallway. "I'm going to take a bath," she flung over her shoulder.

Lyn heard the water running in the tub as she tried to analyze Sam's reaction. It was obvious she was not happy with Lyn's interest in Burne, but how deep did Sam's disapproval go? Would there be serious problems if she let the relationship continue? In spite of the pros and cons that came to mind, the answer eluded her. With a sigh of resignation, she stood up and started toward her bedroom. For the time being, the future would have to take care of itself.

Saturday arrived much too soon although Lyn had everything planned before the big day. She chose chicken for the entrée. The residents of the home were fond of King Ranch Chicken and she thought it would appeal to Burne. A tossed salad, and fresh broccoli should do it. Dessert? Definitely a luscious fruit concoction of some kind.

Burne arrived promptly at six bearing flowers for Lyn and a video for Sam. Sam seemed to be delighted with the gift. She had been saving her allowance to purchase Harry Potter. When she thanked him for the gift, Lyn thought she detected a note of genuine sincerity in her voice.

"The flowers are lovely, Burne. Thank you. Make yourself comfortable," she motioned toward the living room. "I'll put them in water." She returned a few minutes later with the colorful bouquet in a ceramic pitcher and placed it on an antique chest.

Burne was lounging on the sofa, his long legs sprawled out. He came to his feet and went to stand beside her as she rearranged the flowers to her satisfaction. Sam had disappeared into her room with the video.

Lyn turned her head at Burne's approach. He was standing so close their bodies were almost touching. When he reached for her hand, she backed away.

"Lyn, are you afraid of me?" he asked, his voice soft and low.

She tried for a glib answer but decided Burne deserved the truth.

"I guess I am," she admitted, "but not in the way you mean."

"Why don't you tell me how I frighten you?"

Did she imagine the hurt look in his eyes? Looking toward Sam's closed door, she replied, "Maybe later." She stepped around him and walked down the hall to Sam's room. Knocking on the door, she called out, "Sam, dinner's almost ready."

Burne was back on the sofa when she returned to the living room. He grinned as she hurried to the kitchen and, embarrassed at her oversight, stopped to ask, "I'm sorry, would you like something to drink?"

"No, thanks."

She nodded and felt his eyes follow her to the kitchen.

Burne was impressed by the lovely table Lyn had set. The centerpiece of African violets in a ceramic pot lent a dramatic note to the pink place mats and napkins. White iron stone dinnerware and shining stainless flatware created a relaxed atmosphere.

It was a pleasant meal although Lyn had difficulty relaxing. Burne complimented her cooking by saying she was too modest about her skills.

As he leaned away from the table after polishing off the last bite of fresh peach cobbler, he let out a deep breath and sighed.

"It's a good thing I'm not invited to dinner every night. I'd soon be twenty pounds overweight."

Lyn smiled, pleased with the compliment.

"I mean it, Lyn. That was a fabulous meal."

"I'm glad you enjoyed it. Would you like more iced tea?"

"Noooo, I couldn't eat or drink another thing. I may not eat again for a week."

Lyn laughed and Sam giggled. Lyn was proud of Sam's behavior and table manners.

"May I please be excused?" Sam almost bounced out of her chair.

"Yes, you may. Burne, why don't you help her set up the video while I tidy up in here?" She stood and began clearing the table.

"You shouldn't have to do all the work," Burne pushed back his chair. "Let me help, then we can both watch the movie."

"There isn't that much to do. Besides, you are a guest," Lyn admonished.

"Not that kind of guest, I hope." He began to gather up the dishes.

They loaded the dishwasher and cleaned up the kitchen and dining area in a matter of minutes. When Lyn and Burne walked into the living room, Sam was eagerly waiting to start the video. She was sprawled in the only chair facing the TV, leaving the sofa for her mother and Burne. Sitting close together, it was difficult for Lyn to concentrate on the movie. The masculine scent of his cologne mingled with her delicate perfume to create a subtle aura that surrounded them in a sensuous haze.

The show ended and Sam, who had hardly taken her eyes off the screen thereby missing the covert glances and uneasy movements of the two people seated on the sofa, jumped up. "I'm going to call Cathy and tell her all about it."

"No, Sam," Lyn shook her head. "It's much too late. You can tell her tomorrow. It's time for bed now. Remember, you have to get up early for Sunday School." Lyn rose from the sofa.

"Mom! Cathy won't be in bed yet," Sam wheedled as she backed slowly from the room.

Burne came to his feet.

"I said 'no.' Now tell Burne good night."

Sam gave a sigh of resignation. "Good night, Burne. And thanks again for the video. It's neat!"

"I'm glad you like it. Good night, Sam."

"I'll be in to say good night in a few minutes," Lyn called to Sam.

"I know I've told you this before, but she really is a good kid, Lyn."

"Thank you. It's difficult at times, but... I'd better go and tuck her in," she turned and quickly walked away.

Burne resumed his seat on the sofa. When Lyn returned a few minutes later she started toward the chair across from him, but he grabbed her hand and pulled her down beside him.

"You told me earlier this evening that you're afraid of me," Burne reminded her. "What, exactly, did you mean?"

Lyn collected her thoughts and tried to put them in order. She had this crazy idea to tell Burne the circumstances surrounding Sam's birth. It had never mattered in the past what kind of stories other people wanted to fabricate. Somehow, Burne was different. He had never shown the slightest interest in learning about the girl's father.

"Not physically afraid, Burne. It's…it's… I guess you'd say it's an emotional fear."

"Emotional? In what way?" Burne's gray eyes were puzzled.

She didn't look at him but stared straight ahead, her spine stiff, and her hands clasped tightly in her lap. The tension in her body was nearly unbearable, her pulse was beating rapidly and her mouth was dry. Did she really want to reopen all those old wounds and bleed again? It had taken a long time for them to heal before she managed to put them in the past where they belonged. Was it worth the risk?

"It's hard for me to talk about it. It happened a long time ago."

He moved closer to Lyn and gently took her hands in his. She turned to look at him, and her eyes held a far away look as if she had retreated into the past. Sliding his hand up her arm, he drew her into his embrace. She didn't resist but slumped limply against him.

"Lyn," he whispered softly, "You don't have to tell me anything. It doesn't matter. It's in the past. It can't hurt you now."

Lyn drew a ragged breath and sat up but didn't move out of his arms. "I think it would be better if I told you the whole story. Then maybe you will understand how I feel."

"If that's really what you want to do."

She moved to face him and started speaking. "I never dated when I was young. I was too shy to flirt and boys never asked me out. It was the same in college. I concentrated on making good grades. Do you remember I told you I did my internship and graduate work at Kansas State?"

Burne nodded.

"Well, I was just starting the master's program when I met Kevin, a physical therapist at the hospital. He was very good looking, and when he started taking an interest in me, I was on cloud nine. He didn't ask me out right away. We met for coffee or in the cafeteria for lunch. Then, one day, he asked me to go to a movie with him. I was ecstatic. I lived in the dorm on campus, but Kevin had his own apartment," Lyn paused and Burne felt a tremor run through her body.

"You don't have to say any more Lyn. It really doesn't matter," he repeated, his voice gentle and his eyes filled with concern.

"Yes, it does," she insisted. "I want you to know."

Very gently he cupped her chin and turned her head. She looked into his eyes, her own suspiciously wet. He bent his head and touched his lips to hers. She stiffened and tried to pull away, but he held her firmly. His kiss was gentle, without passion, as soft as the touch of a butterfly. Before she could respond, he took his mouth away and she felt bereft.

Catching her breath, she continued, "We went to the movies, and a week later he asked me out again. Afterward, we went to his apartment. I won't go into the ugly details. I'm sure you can figure them out for yourself."

"The bastard! He raped you." Burne's voice was filled with rage and his body stiffened. He clenched his fists.

"No." She shook her head.

Hardly able to contain himself, Burne knew what had happened. "He seduced you." It was a statement not a question.

"Yes."

Her voice was barely audible, and Burne saw tears in her eyes. He ached for the naive young woman she must have been.

"I didn't see him again until I told him I was pregnant. "He ranted and raved and wanted me to have an abortion. He said he would pay for it." Lyn bowed her head and stared unseeingly at the floor.

Burne's hands gripped her shoulders. His voice was tight with anger when he asked, "He didn't offer to marry you?"

"No. I'm not sure I would have married him if he had, but a month later he married someone else."

"My God! No wonder you didn't want to have anything to do with men." He brought her up close and folded her in his arms. She trembled, fighting for control. Gently he caressed her, his hand stroking her back and shoulders with soft light touches.

Lyn, her composure regained, left the haven of his arms and moved to the other end of the sofa. "Now you know what I mean when I say I'm afraid of you."

"Surely you don't think I'm anything like that S.O.B.?" he asked, his voice a harsh rasp.

"No, of course not. But I'm getting to know you, which is something I never did with Kevin. When I told him I was going to have the baby and keep it, he disappeared. I never saw him again."

"Has he ever tried to contact you?" He had to know.

"No," she answered, her voice flat.

Burne disengaged himself and pulled Lyn to her feet. Holding her hands he looked deep into her eyes, his own a stormy gray. "I'm grateful you wanted to tell me all this, but it has no bearing on our relationship. And Lyn, please believe me when I say I would never do anything to hurt either of you."

She took a deep breath and, her voice unsteady, told him, "I want to believe you, but forgive me if I have a problem or two now and then."

"I guess I'll just have to prove my intentions are honorable," he laughed softly.

"Intentions," she squeaked, her eyes wide and staring.

"Yes, intentions. You don't think I'm going to let you get away, do you? I've spent too many years looking for you." He took her in his arms again.

Looking up at him, her mouth agape, she continued to stare at him. *He was serious!* She recovered her voice and stammered, "Things...things are moving too fast. We need more time."

"We have all the time in the world, sweetheart."

At the term of endearment, Lyn blushed and dropped her eyes.

"As much as I hate to, I need to be going. Thank you again for a wonderful dinner."

As she walked with him to the door, Lyn wondered if he would kiss her again. The one brief touch of his lips had been comforting and she wanted to feel them again, but she could not tell him so. Reaching the hallway, he turned and put his arms around her. She made no protest and looked up at him, her lips slightly parted and a message plain n her eyes.

"Lyn." His voice was hoarse with feeling. "I won't deny I want you, but I'm not going to do anything about it. Except this." He bent his head and this time the kiss was everything she hoped for. Caressing her lips gently, his own soft and warm, he outlined her mouth with his tongue. His body was rigid, but his caress was filled with tenderness.

Lyn returned the kiss and knew she was inept. He tightened the embrace and brought her up against him. Tenderly stroking her cheek, he said "I'll call you tomorrow. Good night." He kissed her quickly, opened the door and was gone.

King Ranch Chicken

Serves 6 to 8

3 pounds chicken, cooked, boned and cut up
½ cup chopped onion
½ cup chopped celery
1 teaspoon butter
1 can cream of chicken soup
1 can golden mushroom soup
½ can (4 ozs.) tomatoes and green chilies
1 can (8 ozs.) tomatoes
1 teaspoon salt
1 dozen crisp tortillas, crumbled
1 pound grated cheese

Boil chicken in water until tender. Remove meat from bone and cut into pieces. In skillet sauté onion and celery in butter. Add soups, tomatoes and salt. Heat well. Line 13x9x2 inch dish with crumbled tortillas. Arrange ingredients in layers as follows: tortillas, chicken, soup mixture and cheese. Bake at 350 degrees for 30 minutes.

Peach Cobbler

Serves 6

5 cups sliced peaches (about 8 medium peaches)
1 teaspoon lemon juice
2/3 cup sugar
¼ cup flour
¼ teaspoon cinnamon
¼ teaspoon nutmeg
2 tablespoons butter
Topping
1 cup flour
1/3 cup brown sugar, packed
½ cup butter

Toss peaches with lemon juice. Combine sugar, flour, cinnamon, and nutmeg; mix with peaches. Turn into 8 or 9 inch buttered baking pan. Combine flour and sugar until crumbly. Spread over peaches. Bake at 400 degrees for 30 minutes or until crust is brown and juice is bubbly.

CHAPTER TWELVE

"We didn't lift any prints off the lock, but we didn't expect to," Sergeant Soliz updated Burne over the phone. "We're continuing the background checks, but there are no definite leads yet."

"What's our next move Sergeant?" Burne's question was both personal curiosity and a business necessity.

"When do you take another physical inventory?"

Burne looked at the calendar. "Next week."

"Your super said you usually have Carlos Romero help you with it. That right?"

"Yeah. He's familiar with the stock, and it makes the job a little easier."

"How about the deliveries? You ever check the stuff in yourself?"

"Not unless I happen to be there when a truck comes in. Then I might do it to help Dan out." Burne doodled on the scratch pad in front of him.

"Do you have a schedule of all the deliveries?" Soliz questioned.

"Sure. That's all in the computer."

"Good. Here's what we'd like for you to do. Check in all the deliveries personally, say for a couple of weeks. Make a note of your observations, the drivers, the amount of materials on the trucks, etc. We'll go over everything with you before you start. Think you can arrange it?"

"Sure. That's no problem considering the system we use," Burne glanced down at the scratch pad and saw he had written Lyn's name several times. He grinned and shook his head, forcing his mind back to the conversation with the sergeant. "You don't think the vendors are involved, do you?"

"We don't know, but we don't want to overlook any possibilities."

"I'll talk to Dan." Burne dropped the pencil and straightened in his chair. "When do you want me to start?"

"Let's wait until after you take the next inventory. If you could help us out for a full period between checks, that would give us more to go on."

"The computer is set up for a monthly check. I can take the regular one next week, take care of the deliveries then do another one."

"Good idea. I'll pass this on and get back to you. And, thanks Mr. MacKenzie. We appreciate your help."

"Glad to do it. You guys have a rough job."

"I wish more of our citizens felt that way. I'll be in touch."

Burne hung up, pondering Soliz's plan. It would tie him a little tighter to the job site, but that's what he was getting paid for. And a hefty salary it was, too. Ample enough to support a wife and family. His thoughts skittered to a halt. Wife and family? He grew pensive. Was he in love with Lyn? He had told her his intentions were honorable. Taking her to bed without the benefit of marriage was out of the question.

The other side of the coin was her experience with Sam's father. Would she be able to overcome her inhibitions? Would she cling to her fears and be frigid? Her response to his kisses was timid and inexperienced. He couldn't decide if there was passion under her cool exterior. Oh, hell, it didn't do any good to speculate! He had told her they had plenty of time to explore their feelings, and he would keep his word.

* * *

Shades of red and gold, orange and yellow, colored the sky as the dying sun faded from the horizon. Daylight was replaced by a lavender tint that slowly turned to purple and twilight descended over the hilly landscape. Lyn, sitting on the apartment's small patio that opened off the dining area, tried to clear her mind of the disturbing thoughts that occupied it. She had not seen Burne since the night he came to dinner although he had called her several times. He explained he was having some problems at the job site.

She picked up the glass of iced tea from the table beside her and slowly sipped from it. Janie Mertz, the night shift receptionist, said he had visited his father one evening when Janie was on duty. Had she scared him off with her confession about Sam's birth? Did a ten-year old child take the romance out of a relationship? Was he having second thoughts about a ready-made family? All the negative reasons raced around in her head like so many mice in a maze.

"Mom," Sam called from inside. "I need some help."

Her daughter's voice broke into her troubled thoughts, bringing a welcome respite. With a sigh, Lyn returned to the dining area where Sam was struggling with a craft project.

"Would you hold this, please, while I put some glue on it?" Sam was making a log cabin, which would be part of a frontier village. They worked together for several minutes. Sam, her hands sticky with glue, jumped up from the table. "Can I watch the video after I get this glue off?"

"May I," corrected Lyn automatically.

"May I, p-l-e-a-s-e?"

"Not tonight, Sam. It would be too late when it's over."

Sam grimaced but did not insist. "When is Burne coming again?"

"I don't know. He's very busy with his work." Lyn cleared away Sam's mess thereby avoiding looking at her.

Sam watched her mother, her eyes narrowed and her gaze speculative. "Maybe he won't come back any more."

Lyn gasped in total surprise. "Why do you say that?" she managed to ask.

"Well…Susie said he wouldn't want a wife who already had a kid, especially one who doesn't have a father." Sam kept her eyes focused on her mother's face.

Lyn's breath caught in her throat. She had tried to spare Sam as much as possible, but there were times when she was powerless to shield her from hurt. She gathered the girl close and hugged her tightly. "Oh, Sam! You know we've talked about this many times." The tears she struggled to hold back threatened to overflow, and she felt as if her heart was being torn from her chest.

"It's okay, Mom. We don't need him. Besides, I don't like Burne all that much."

Lyn dropped her arms and stepped back. "Sam! He has been very nice to you ——taking you to Sea World, out to eat and giving you a video."

"Yeah, but that was because he was trying to make out with you." Sam stuck out her bottom lip in defiance.

Lyn's face paled, but her blue eyes blazed. "Where did you hear talk like that, young lady?"

"Well…Susie said it and so did Juanita."

"It wasn't a very nice thing to say, and I don't want to hear you repeat it, *ever*." Lyn knew the girls had heard the remark from grown-ups, but she didn't want Sam to dwell on it. People were going to talk no matter what a person did or did not do.

Trouble seemed to come in bunches like grapes. A private luncheon to be hosted by one of the residents was canceled after the special foods were ordered. Gertrude fell in the kitchen and sprained her ankle. She went on sick leave for a week. One of the ovens malfunctioned, and the menus had to be adjusted while it was being repaired.

What will happen next? Lyn was bone tired from the long days and not enough rest. After Kevin, she had sworn she would never let another man cause her sleepless nights. Not that she did not sleep, she defended herself, but it was a restless and dream-filled slumber that left her feeling tired and edgy.

The phone erupted in a loud jangling that startled her from her lethargic state. "Dining Services, Lyn DeVinney."

"Hello, Lyn. It's Burne. I called you at home but there was no answer. Aren't you working awfully late?"

Lyn's throat was suddenly dry and her heart thudded in her chest. "Some…sometimes it's necessary," her voice was unsteady.

"Don't I know it!"

"I'm sure you do," she replied dryly.

Burne caught the change in her tone immediately. "What's wrong, Lyn?"

"Nothing, why?"

"You don't sound like yourself. Is there a problem of some kind?"

Lyn sighed and leaned back in her chair. "I'm just tired, that's all. Several things have gone wrong the past few days, and I've had to work late."

"Sorry, to hear that. Problems seem to come with the territory, don't they?" Burne thought about the police investigation.

"Yes, they, do!"

"Would you like to do something Saturday? Go to a movie, take Sam to the zoo? We can do whatever you want."

Lyn took a deep breath and thought about her answer. She did not want to seem too eager. "I really need to do some things in the apartment."

"Lyn, something is wrong! Why won't you tell me what is bothering you? Maybe I can help," he pleaded.

She heard the anxiety in his voice and wanted to believe him. "It's nothing really. I need to pick up Sam. Why don't you come by Saturday afternoon about two o'clock. The pool is open and I hear you like to swim."

"That sounds good to me. Afterward I'll take you and Sam out to dinner. Okay?"

"Yes. We'll see you Saturday."

"Say hello to Sam for me."

"I will."

"Good night."

* * *

Bright sunshine reflected off the water, and it became a dazzling blue sea with a pebbled concrete beach. Tables with colorful umbrella tops, chairs and lounges were scattered around the edge of the pool. Lyn, her fair skin a perfect target for the greedy sun, sat in the shade covered with sunscreen, while Burne and Sam cavorted in the water. They had joined a group of swimmers playing water tag. It was obvious Sam was enjoying herself as she tagged Burne and swam away. Even though the girl was an excellent swimmer, Lyn was touched that he was protective of her.

The game broke up and Burne climbed out of the pool. He ran his hand through his wet hair as he walked toward her. Lyn felt a flutter in the pit of her stomach as she surveyed his lithe form in the tight black swim trunks. He was not particularly muscular, but his body was well proportioned. A broad chest, narrow waist and long legs attested to his male attributes.

Reaching for a towel, he grinned and told her, "You don't know what you're missing. That was great!"

"Oh, yes I do! I'm missing a great sunburn." She sat up and swung her legs over the edge of the lounge.

"Don't you ever go in the water?"

"Of course, but I swim after the sun goes down. The pool is open until ten o'clock."

"I'll remember that," he said, his voice husky.

"Why?"

"A late night swim is always a good way to end a romantic evening." His grin challenged her to reply.

Lyn's face grew hot and she swallowed the comment on the end of her tongue. *Yes, and you've probably had plenty of experience!*

Draping the towel around his neck, he sat in a chair beside her. "I think I'll head for Dad's place. I left a change of clothes there. Will an hour give you girls enough time?"

"I think so." Lyn stood and began gathering up their paraphernalia.

"You pick the place to eat. And, remember, I've worked up quite an appetite."

Lyn paused, considering for a moment, then offered, "There are some really good German restaurants in Fredericksburg. It's only a short drive from Mt. Laurel."

"Sounds good to me. I'll see you in an hour." He touched her face with his fingertips and ran them down her cheek. His gray eyes darkened to pewter, and Lyn thought she saw desire flicker for a moment before he turned away.

After a delicious meal of authentic German food, they spent an hour looking through the shops in the restored settlement. Lyn loved antiques and had managed to collect a few good pieces. Her dream, which she never shared with anyone except her family, was to own a restored Victorian home and fill it with period pieces. "You really go for that stuff, don't you?" Burne had noticed the knowledge she displayed when talking with the shopkeepers about their wares.

"Yes, I love to browse through the shops. Most of the pieces are much too expensive for me, but I have found some things at estate sales."

"Is that a pastime of yours? Going to estate sales?"

"When I can find the time, yes. Sam likes them too. There are always a lot of interesting old things for her to poke through."

The silence lengthened as they drove toward Mt. Laurel. Glancing in the rear-view mirror, Burne saw that Sam was sound asleep. He turned to Lyn and nodded toward the back seat. "Our girl has gone to sleep on us," he grinned.

She caught the reference to 'our girl.' His interest in Sam seemed too genuine to be faked. Lyn's heart did a flip flop in her chest. His effect on her emotions was becoming more and more potent. Was she in love with him? She did not know. The brief infatuation with Kevin bore no resemblance to her feelings for Burne.

"Yes, Sam has no difficulty sleeping," she answered. Before she could stop them, the words were out of her mouth. "I should be so lucky!"

Burne's eyebrows rose, and he turned to look at her for a brief moment. "You have trouble sleeping?"

Lyn searched frantically for a non-committal reply. "Doesn't everybody?"

"Yes, but there's usually a good reason for it. What's keeping you awake, Lyn?"

"Oh, the usual things. My job, Sam's well-being," she tried for a casual tone.

"From what I see, you do an excellent job, but I know responsibility can get you down. As for Sam, I don't think you have anything to worry about. She seems very well-adjusted," he tried to reassure her.

"Yes, but there are always new problems cropping up and sometimes they're not easily solved."

"It's all part of life, Lyn. We just do the best we can." He reached for her hand and urged her closer to his side. She did not resist and allowed him to embrace her.

"How do you feel about a late night swim?"

"Tonight?"

"Yes, tonight. I haven't been alone with you all day."

Common sense told her to make some kind of excuse. Did she not always use common sense and rarely give way to impulse? Feeling young and giddy, she laughed softly. "Let me get Sam settled and I'll join you at the pool."

Sam grumbled when they woke her but went docilely along with Lyn to the apartment. In a matter of minutes, she was in bed and back to sleep.

Lyn donned her still damp suit and giggled when she thought of Burne changing clothes in the back of the Suburban. Grabbing a couple of towels from the linen closet, she hurried to join him.

The pool was brightly lit, but the grassy area surrounding it was filled with shadows. There were no other swimmers, and they had the place to themselves. Burne was already in the water and swimming fast laps the length of the pool. He stood up and beckoned to her. She entered from the opposite end, swam to where Burne was waiting, and rose to a standing position in front of him. The water was running down her body as smooth as rain on window glass. Her fair skin gleamed like marble under the bright lights. Drops of moisture clung to her eyelashes and turned her eyes into sparkling sapphires.

He took a step nearer and reached out to her. She lifted her arms and their hands touched. He gently pulled her to him, and his arms enfolded her in a loose embrace. Cupping her face between his hands, he placed a soft kiss on her parted lips. With what little skill she possessed, Lyn kissed him back.

A shudder ran through his body, and he tore his mouth away while his hands gripped her shoulders. His breathing ragged, he released her and moved back a step. "Lord, woman, don't do that to me!"

His voice penetrated her dream-like state and reality came flooding back. They were standing under the bright lights, plainly visible to anyone watching from the apartments. She turned and swam toward the deep end of the pool. The water cooled her burning cheeks, and she surfaced to see Burne swimming along side her. She could not look at him and climbed out of the pool to find him already out of the water.

Without a word, he guided her across the concrete into the shadows. "There are things we need to talk about, and I know you don't want an audience." She started to speak but he held a finger to her lips. "I'm sorry I had to stop you honey, but a man can only stand so much."

Lyn, her whole being aflame with embarrassment, was glad for the darkness. "I'm sorry. I thought you wanted me to kiss you."

The hurt in her voice tore at his gut. "Oh, honey, I do, but not when we're half-naked and in plain sight. I don't want people to get the wrong idea."

In spite of the warmth of the summer evening, Lyn felt chilled. Fool! She was a thirty-three year old woman who did not possess the knowledge of a teenager.

"Especially since I'm a woman with an illegitimate child," she responded bitterly.

"Oh, sweetheart, that isn't what I meant." Burne reached for her hand, but she drew away. "Please, Lyn, don't be angry with me. What can I say to convince you that I really care about you?"

Taking a deep breath she exhaled slowly, trying to recover her composure. "I'm angry at myself." When Burne opened his mouth to protest, she shook her head. "No. I think enough has been said for tonight."

CHAPTER THIRTEEN

The lettering on the truck door read, "River City Hardware & Tool Supply, Inc." Clipboard in hand, the driver jumped down from the cab. He was a slender man of medium height with a closely trimmed beard and shoulder length brown hair. In jeans, boots and a straw hat, he looked more like a cowboy than a truck driver.

Burne, watching from the office window, saw the truck pull in. "That River City delivery we've been expecting just came in," he told Andy.

The project engineer, intent on the information flashing across the computer screen, looked up, his expression blank.

"I'm going out to check it in," Burne told him.

Comprehension dawned and Andy stammered, "Oh, yeah, well, I'll hold down the fort." His attention was back on the computer before Burne closed the door.

Burne chuckled thinking about how Andy could lose track of time, people, places and things when his engineer's mind was focused on a complicated construction technique. He'd bet Shelley would be having dinner with only Amy for company for the next few nights. Both he and Andy had been staying late, setting up temporary procedures to help the San Antonio Police Department.

Dan and the driver were going over the delivery receipts when Burne reached the tool sheds. Dan made a quick introduction, and Burne learned the driver's name was Ray Flowers.

"Where's Carlos?" Flowers asked, darting quick glances around the site.

"He was needed in another area today." Dan answered. "Burne is going to check the stuff in. Thanks for the help, Burne."

"Any time, Dan," Burne told him. He turned his attention to the driver who seemed nervous as he started toward the back of the truck. A half-hour later, Flowers climbed back into the cab and left the site. When Burne returned to the office with copies of the delivery receipts, Andy was reaching for his hardhat.

"How'd it go?" he inquired.

"Okay," Burne replied, dropping the papers on his desk. "The driver, his name's Flowers, seemed kinda jumpy, though."

"You think the back orders have anything to do with it?" Andy paused at the door.

"I don't know. Guess we'll just have to wait and see how the inventory turns out."

Sitting down at the computer, he pulled up the program. The new stock had to be entered, and the records brought up-to-date. It took longer to accomplish, because he found an error in the previous entry. This prompted him to run a complete check on the file. The discrepancies varied little, but the small amounts were beginning to add up to a nice little haul for somebody. Flowers' behavior nagged at him, but there was nothing he could put his finger on. He stood, stretched and rubbed the back of his neck.

"I'm about ready to call it a day," Andy said as he entered the office and shut the door behind him.

"Me, too. I need some exercise. Think I'll head for the club and a good long swim." Burne began clearing his desk.

When Burne walked into the pool area, the first person he saw was Paul Mansfield. He was sitting at the shallow end of the pool talking with another man. Paul threw up his hand. Fifteen minutes later as Burne was climbing out of the water Mansfield's companion was gone, and he sauntered to Burne's side.

"How's it going, Mr. MacKenzie?"

"Okay. How about you?" Burne picked up his towel and began to dry off.

"Things have been a little hectic at The Manor. You know, with Lyn being off and all." Paul sat down and let his feet trail in the water.

Burne stopped abruptly, the towel hanging limply in his hand. "Lyn isn't sick is she?" he asked, his anxiety obvious.

"Didn't you know? Sam is the one who's sick."

Burne felt a sharp stab of guilt. He hadn't called Lyn since the scene at the swimming pool. He felt she needed time to sort out her feelings and, he admitted, his pride had been wounded.

"Do you know what the problem is?" He finished drying off and draped the towel around his neck.

"No. She has a high fever from what I hear, and there's some talk about bringing her to a hospital in San Antonio."

"Good Lord! Lyn must be frantic." Burne suppressed the desire to jump up and go to her immediately.

"Yes, but at least her parents are in town."

"Lyn never mentioned her parents to me. I just assumed they live in San Antonio."

"They do," Paul answered, "but they travel a lot and have been gone for a couple of months."

Burne sensed a change in Mansfield's attitude. He seemed to imply that he was privy to the details of Lyn's private life whereas she had shared little with Burne. "I'm sure they're a big help to her." He sat down beside Mansfield.

"Yes and so are Rhonda and Bob."

Burne was ignorant of who Rhoda and Bob might be.

Paul turned his head slightly, and when he spoke his tone was condescending. "Rhonda and Bob are Lyn's sister and brother-in-law."

"I see." Burne pretended to ignore the smirk on the chef's face.

Back in the apartment a half-hour later, Burne dialed Lyn's number. He decided Sam had been admitted to the hospital when Lyn answered on the fifth ring. "Lyn, it's Burne. I just learned that Sam is ill."

"Yes, she is," her voice was low and ragged.

"Is there anything I can do?" Burne gripped the receiver and held his breath.

Forgetting their strained relationship, Lyn answered, "I don't think so. If she isn't better by morning, the doctor wants to admit her to the hospital in San Antonio."

"Have they made a diagnosis yet?" A pain-like sensation centered in his chest, and he realized Sam meant a great deal to him. "Is it too late for me to come to Mt. Laurel?"

Lyn was silent for a moment before she answered. "The doctor is not allowing visitors until we know more about her illness."

"Is there anybody there with you?" He wanted to hold and comfort her.

"No. My parents left about an hour ago."

"I'll be there in twenty minutes," he wasn't asking for permission.

A minute after Lyn answered his knock, Burne was inside and she was in his arms. Her body was limp with exhaustion, and she buried her face against his chest. Holding her tightly, he tried to find words of comfort. He body trembled as she struggled for control.

"Everything is going to be all right, Lyn. I promise." He prayed he was not offering false hope.

She raised her head, her eyes wet with unshed tears. Her pretty features were drawn and lined with fatigue. He wished with all his heart he could take her pain away. She was so strong, accepting her responsibilities, never expecting or asking for help, he wanted to share her burden. Like a neon sign inside his head, the words flashed across his brain. He loved her! This independent courageous woman had become the most important person in his world.

Burne bent his head and placed a soft kiss on her forehead as his fingertips brushed her tears away. Leading her to the sofa, he seated her gently. He pulled a handkerchief from his pocket and silently handed it to her.

She accepted it and dabbed at her eyes. "Thank you," her voice was barely above a whisper.

He nodded but said nothing. She needed time to bring her shattered emotions under control.

"I'm sorry. It's just been so...so ..."

He gathered her back into his arms. "I know, sweetheart, I know," he told her, stroking her back with gentle hands. Her body slowly relaxed, and she leaned against him.

"Do you feel like talking about it?" he asked.

She nodded. "She complained of feeling *icky* but didn't want to stay home from the center. When Janet picked them up that afternoon, Sam said she had a headache and Janet gave her Tylenol. She didn't eat anything that evening, and the next morning she had a fever. I didn't go in to work, and that afternoon I took her to the doctor. He said it was a bug of some kind and gave me a prescription. She's been taking the medication for two days, but her fever hasn't gone down. They did some blood work but the results haven't come back."

The effort seemed to drain her energy and she sagged against him. Why had her parents left her to fight this battle alone?

As if she could read his mind, she told him, "I sent Mom and Dad home. They were here all day. My mother has a heart condition and shouldn't overdo."

"How about you? Have you been able to get any sleep?"

"I'm all right. I slept a few hours last night."

"Very few, I'm willing to bet." He stroked the top of her head.

She gave him a wan smile. "Thank you for coming, Burne."

"I just wish you had called me. Mansfield told me when I met him at the club this evening."

"I thought maybe you had gone to the Manor to see your father." She snuggled into his embrace.

"No," his arms tightened around her. "I haven't seen Dad for a week. I haven't been able to get away early."

Sounds were coming from Sam's room, and Lyn jumped to her feet. "She must be awake." With Burne at her heels, she hurried down the hall.

Burne stopped just inside the doorway, but he could see Sam tossing about on the bed.

Lyn tried to soothe her, the words inaudible. Taking a plastic pan from the bedside table, she motioned for Burne to come forward.

"Would you mind getting me a fresh pan of water and adding a few ice cubes to it? She needs to be sponged off." Her voice quivered slightly, and Burne knew her control was strained to the limit.

He took the pan, glancing at Sam as he turned away. The girl was lying on her back, her dark hair fanned out on the pillow. Her pallor was ghostly and moisture beaded on her face. There was no doubt she was very sick. When he returned, Lyn seemed a bit flustered as she dropped a washcloth into the pan. It took him a minute to realize she wanted him to leave the room while she tended to Sam.

"Call me if you need anything," he told her.

Burne went back to the living room and flopped down on the sofa but found it impossible to concentrate on the evening paper. After what seemed an eternity, Lyn joined him. "How is she?"

"I think she's a little more comfortable. She woke up and wanted a drink of water. She's asleep now."

"Lyn," Burne came to his feet and looked down at her. "I know you're going to object, but I want to stay with you tonight. You shouldn't be alone."

Lyn sat up straight, her eyes wide. "I can't let you do that," she told him.

"You have a very sick child and you need help. Under the circumstance, I don't think we should worry about propriety." His eyes were focused intently on her.

"I appreciate your offer, Burne, I really do, but…" her voice choked up.

He drew her to her feet and held her hands. "Listen to me Lyn. I know my timing stinks, but I have to tell you now. I love you, and I want to take care of you and Sam."

She collapsed against him and great choking sobs shook her body. Burne held her and gently stroked her back while her tears soaked the front of his shirt.

When she quieted, he lifted her head and looked into her eyes. "I picked a poor time to declare myself, didn't I?" he said ruefully.

Tears clinging to her lashes, she took the damp handkerchief he offered. "Oh, no, Burne! It's just that…that I didn't think you really…cared."

"Lady, you don't know your own charm. I guess that's one of the reasons I love you. You're so honest with no false pretenses."

Her arms encircled his neck; he bent his head and their lips met. The kiss was gentle and sweet, without passion, but full of promise.

Lyn finally agreed that Burne could spend the night, and he convinced her to relax in a hot bath. She came back into the room dressed in a long pale blue robe, and Burne's breath stuck in his throat. Her honey-blond hair curled softly around her face, and her fair skin was free of make-up. She looked as fragile and delicate as the child in the bedroom.

"Mom!" Sam's voice broke the spell.

"I'm right here, Sam," Lyn hurried to Sam's bedside, Burne following close behind.

"I'm thirsty," Sam complained, her voice weak and raspy.

"Do you think you could drink some juice?"

"I think so," she replied as she struggled to sit up. Sam looked beyond Lyn at Burne who stood watching from the doorway. "Burne did you come to see me?"

Moving to the bedside, he took her hand in his. It was hot to the touch. "Yes, I did. We have to get you well. We have a lot of things to do this summer."

Sam smiled, a remnant of her mischievous grin. "Can I wear my uniform?"

Burned laughed and, smoothing her hair back from her face, answered, "Sure. It looks great on you."

Sam managed a weak giggle.

Lyn returned with a glass of orange juice. Sam drank half of it. She sighed with the effort, closed her eyes and drifted off to sleep. Lyn and Burne tiptoed quietly from the room.

"Why don't you try to get some rest? I'll sit with Sam," he hugged her to his side.

"No, I couldn't sleep."

Burne sensed Lyn was uncomfortable, but it secretly pleased him that she had not shared her life with another man. The circumstances surrounding Sam's birth hardly qualified her as an experienced woman. "At least try," he coaxed.

Exhaustion was claiming her tired body. Taking a pillow and blanket from the linen closet, she spread them on the sofa. "Sam will probably sleep for hours. You should get some sleep yourself."

Burne's eyes were drawn to her body although she was covered from head to toe. In spite of his efforts, desire sizzled through his blood. *MacKenzie, you're sick!* His brain kept repeating now was not the time, but his body refused to listen. He dared not touch her or he would be lost.

Burne's behavior had changed, and Lyn was puzzled. His face had a strained expression, and he was holding his arms rigidly at his sides.

"What's wrong, Burne? Do you want to leave? You really don't have to stay, you know."

"Go to bed, Lyn. I'll call you if I need you." His voice was harsh.

Lyn's face colored a bright pink. For a long moment she looked at him, her eyes searching his face. Without a word, she turned and left the room.

Burne let out the pent up breath he was holding. Abruptly he sat down on the sofa and hung his head. Running his hands through his hair, he cursed to himself. *Damn!* He had never had this problem before.

Sam was restless, and Burne soothed her with soft words and cold cloths on her forehead. Only once during the night did she call out. Burne hurried to her bedside and, when she saw him, she stuttered, "I...I want Mom."

"She's asleep, honey. What do you need?"

She didn't answer, and it finally penetrated Burne's thick head that Sam was suffering from embarrassment.

"I…I need to…I need to go to the bathroom."

It was Burne's turn to be embarrassed. "In that case, I'd better wake your mother." He hurried from the room.

Lyn had left her door open, and the room was dark. Soft moonlight streamed in the windows and played hide and seek with the shadows. As Burne approached the sleeping woman, her face was illuminated in the half-light.

Her features were relaxed, her skin pale and smooth, her lips slightly parted. With all the will power he possessed, Burne kept a tight rein on his control. "Lyn," he called softly. She stirred but did not waken. He leaned closer. "Lyn," he repeated. Placing his mouth close to her ear, he whispered once more, "Lyn, wake up. Sam needs you."

He had said the magic words. Her eyes flew open, and she sat up as her sleep-drugged brain began to function. She jumped out of bed and started towards Sam's room, but she stepped back and reached for the robe lying on the foot of the bed. The moonlight streaming into the room outlined her slender figure through the sheer fabric of her gown. His control strained to the limit, he stood rooted to the floor. Lyn, unaware of the battle he was fighting, left the room at a run.

A persistent knocking at the door brought Burne out of a deep sleep that had finally claimed him in the wee hours of the morning. He sat up, trying to clear the cobwebs from his brain. Evidently Lyn was sleeping soundly and had not heard it. He was still wearing his jeans and shirt but had taken off his shoes. Giving no thought as to whom the early morning visitor might be, he opened the door wide. A man and woman, both gray-haired and casually dressed, stood before him. His quizzical look slowly changed to one of comprehension. Lyn's parents had come to check on Sam!

CHAPTER FOURTEEN

"What's going on here?" the man asked, his tone hostile. "Who are you and what are you doing in my daughter's apartment?"

Lyn's parents! How was he going to explain being there at eight o'clock in the morning?

"I'm Burne MacKenzie. Maybe you'd better come inside. It's not at all what it seems."

"I should hope not!" Lyn's mother replied, her voice indignant. The resemblance between mother and daughter was obvious. Mrs. DeVinney's blond hair was liberally streaked with gray giving it a frosted appearance.

Burne stepped back and the couple walked into the room. Lyn chose that moment to appear, wearing the robe from the previous evening.

"I thought I heard voices. Mom, Dad, you're here early." She smiled, her eyes puffy from sleep.

"Lyn, what is going on here?" her father demanded.

"Oh, dear! How do I explain? Burne…he…he…"

Burne moved to her side and slipped an arm around her waist. "It's simple. I'm in love your daughter and I want to marry her," he said flatly.

"Marry?" The elder DeVinneys reacted as if he had said they were taking the next shuttle to the moon.

Lyn tilted her head and looked into Burne's face. His gray eyes were dark with feeling. He still held her. She smiled at him, and his heart thudded in his chest. Oblivious to his audience, he lowered his head and touched her lips in a brief kiss. Her face colored a fiery red, and she stepped out of his embrace.

"I'll make some coffee, then we can talk. Have you had breakfast?" She directed the question toward her parents.

"Yes. How is Sam this morning?" Mrs. DeVinney asked, looking toward Sam's bedroom.

"She was sleeping when I peaked in a minute ago." Lyn replied as she made her way to the kitchen.

Mrs. DeVinney followed right behind her, and Burne knew she was primed for action. Lyn's father was staring at the sofa where the tangled bedding gave evidence that someone had been sleeping there.

"I came to see Lyn last evening and, when I saw how exhausted she was, I insisted on staying."

"Why is it that Lyn has never mentioned you? If you plan to be married, you must have known each other for awhile."

"Burne," Lyn interrupted from the dining area where she was setting the table. "Do you need to call your office?"

"Yes, I should. Thanks for reminding me."

After giving Manuel a message for Andy, Burne turned his attention back to Lyn's father. He was of medium height, his dark hair sprinkled with gray, and deep blue eyes, which, evidently, his daughter had inherited.

Lyn stuck her head in the living room. "Can you stay for breakfast?"

"Yes. I'm not about to pass up an invitation like that," Burne replied.

"That's the least I can do after you were up all night with Sam." Lyn hurried back to the kitchen.

"You took care of Sam?" Lyn's father asked, sounding surprised.

"I don't know how good a job I did, but Lyn needed the rest. She was worn out."

While the elder DeVinneys took only coffee, Burne enjoyed fluffy scrambled eggs and crisp bacon. He listened as Lyn attempted to fill in the gaps in their story. A grin creased his bristly features as she tried, tactfully, to tell them about his father's dissatisfaction with The Manor. He interrupted to say their initial meetings had sparked his interest in her.

"She gave me a hard time," he complained, but his voice held a warmth that said it was well worth the effort.

"You were very persistent," she reminded him.

Looking from her daughter to the man who had broken down barriers she thought were insurmountable, Mrs. DeVinney raised the question that was uppermost in Burne's mind. "What are your plans?"

"Mom!" Sam called loudly.

Lyn was on her feet in an instant with her mother not far behind. They found Sam sitting up in bed.

"Oh, honey, how are you feeling?" Lyn took her daughter's hand.

"I'm hungry," Sam complained.

Lyn felt her forehead and found it cool to the touch. Hugging her daughter tightly, she gave a silent prayer of thanksgiving. The fever had broken.

"Burne, were you here last night?" Sam questioned.

Lyn looked up to see Burne and her father standing in the doorway.

"Yes. Looks like you're feeling better."

"Yeah. Did you take care of me?"

Burne, somewhat embarrassed, nodded. "I gave you a drink of water a couple of times."

Sam's brow puckered and she frowned. "I remember cold wash cloths on my face. And I had to go to the bathroom." She grinned. "You went and got Mom."

Burne was saved from replying when her stomach emitted a loud growl.

"Sounds like one little girl needs to eat." Her grandmother laughed. "You stay with her, Lyn, and I'll fix something."

"Thanks, Mom."

Mr. DeVinney, who hadn't spoken, came forward and hugged Sam. "I'm glad you're better, Punkin. You had us worried."

"I'm sorry, Grandpa," Sam told him as she returned the hug.

"Lyn," Burne spoke up, "I have to be going. I need to stop at my apartment before I go to the job site," he said, rubbing the stubble on his jaw.

"I'm sorry you didn't get much sleep last night. You should have let me tend Sam."

"Don't worry about it. I was glad to help." He walked to the bed and, reaching out, touched Sam on the shoulder. "I'm very glad you're feeling better. Get lots of rest and mind your mother." He grinned and gave her a mock salute as he left the room.

"I'm going to see Burne out. I'll be right back," Lyn called over her shoulder as she followed Burne down the hallway.

Reaching the door, Burne turned and gathered her into his arms. "Now that I've declared myself before God and your parents, do you think you could give me a goodbye kiss?"

She did not answer but put her arms around his neck, went up on tiptoes and pressed her lips to his. In spite of an aching back from the too-short sofa, Burne's pulse speeded up, and the room was suddenly too warm. He returned her kiss but tamped down the desire to ravage her mouth. Gently, he disengaged her arms and set her away from him. "I have to go. Please give your parents my excuses."

Lyn gulped in a breath of air and managed to answer, "Yes, they'll understand."

"I'll call you later." A brush of his lips against hers, and the door closed behind him.

* * *

Arriving at the job site, Burne found Andy primed and ready. "Who is she?"

Burne grinned and decided it was time to fill in the blanks for Andy, but he did not want to make it too easy. "Her name is Sam and she's ten years old."

As he expected, he had thrown Andy a curve, and the engineer gaped at him. "Her name is Sam and she's ten years old," he repeated, his voice ending on a high note.

Burne laughed and took pity on his friend. He quickly related the barest details concerning Lyn and Sam, omitting her reluctance to go out with him, Sam's parentage and his proposal.

"Wait till I tell Shelley!" Andy could hardly contain himself.

"Well, aren't you two always trying to fix me up with someone?"

Andy ignored Burne's teasing remark. "Why don't you bring her to dinner. You know we'd love to meet her."

Burne grinned. "Yes, I know your curiosity is killing you, but hadn't you better ask Shelley first? Then I'll ask Lyn."

Andy reluctantly agreed that was the best approach.

Burne gave himself a mental shake. He had too many other things to think about to be concerned with Andy's curiosity. The most important by far was his proposal. Lyn hadn't really given him an answer, and he knew it would be unfair to press her now with Sam's illness uppermost in her mind. Deep in thought, he didn't realize somebody had entered the office until Andy spoke.

"What can I do for you, Sergeant?"

With a nod toward Manuel's vacant desk, the detective asked, "He out to lunch?"

"Yeah," Andy replied.

"We got an anonymous tip about the thefts you reported," Soliz revealed.

Burne forced his attention to the problems at hand, pushed away from his desk and got to his feet. "Who is it?" he asked.

Soliz grinned, his normally taciturn features pleasantly altered. "Not so fast. I said 'tip.' We need to check it out first."

Burne nodded. "Yeah, I can understand that." He motioned toward the coffee pot. "Could you use a cup of coffee?" He poured himself a mug.

Soliz shook his head. "No, thanks." He seated himself next to Burne's desk. "The first thing we need is an up-to-date inventory check to compare with the older ones that show discrepancies. When we have that information, we will be sure of our next move."

"I can have it for you by tomorrow," Burne told him, taking a sip of the strong brew.

"That's good enough." Soliz reached for a cigarette.

"Can you tell us anything at all?" Andy questioned as he helped himself to the coffee.

"Not right now. As I said, it was anonymous, and most of the time that kind of information is not reliable. Sometimes it's done to throw suspicion away from the real thieves." He exhaled a stream of smoke through his nostrils.

"Makes sense," Burne admitted. He sat on a corner of his desk, his mind going to the nervous truck driver, Flowers. No need to mention it, he had nothing to base his feelings on. "You want me to call you when I get the results of the inventory check?"

"Yeah," Soliz came to his feet. "We'll need printouts too. In the meantime, I want to talk with Potts. Is he around?"

"He's probably having lunch about now, but he should be on the site. Dan rarely goes out to eat," Andy volunteered.

With a nod, the detective headed for the door.

* * *

Lyn telephoned the doctor's office to report that Sam was improving.

"That's good news. Sometimes these bugs are hard to explain. Be sure she takes all of the antibiotics and gets plenty of rest," the doctor instructed.

"I will, doctor. She's going to stay with my parents in San Antonio for a few days. Mom will fuss over her like a mother hen."

"A little coddling isn't going to hurt her. She's been a mighty sick little girl. Now, if there is a change, say her fever returns, call us right away. If she has no complications, bring her to the office in about a week. We want to keep tabs on her."

"Thank you, doctor."

While Lyn prepared lunch, Mrs. DeVinney helped Sam pack her bag. Lyn needed to get back to The Manor, but Sam was not well enough to go to the center. She was going to spend a few days with her grandparents, which delighted them.

"Sam, do you like Mr. MacKenzie?" her grandmother asked.

"Well, I didn't at first. It's always been just Mom and me, you know, but now...."

"I know dear, but you need to think about your mother. You will grow up, go away to college and get married. Then she will be alone." Mrs. DeVinney continued to fold Sam's clothing.

"I never thought about that." Sam's expression grew pensive and a frown puckered her brow.

"There was no reason to before, but now you do need to think about it." She turned to face Sam.

Sam was silent for a long moment, then, her tone solemn, replied, "He must like me a lot and not just want Mom."

"Of course he likes you. He wouldn't have taken care of you if he didn't." Her grandmother smiled warmly.

Sam grinned. "He likes baseball, too. And Sea World."

"Hey, you two! I've been calling you. Lunch is ready," Lyn spoke from the doorway.

"Grandma and I had things to talk about," Sam replied, rising to her feet.

"We certainly did," Mrs. DeVinney responded, giving Sam a hug.

* * *

After a late dinner, Lyn and Burne went back to the apartment.

"I'm going to pick up Sam tomorrow night after the meeting," Lyn told him as he unlocked her door.

"It was good of your folks to look after her for a few days."

They stepped inside, and he pulled her to him for a quick kiss. "We have a lot of things to talk about."

"Yes," Lyn agreed as she fastened the security chain. She was anxious to begin the discussion; at the same time she was reluctant. She had not given Burne an answer to his proposal, and she was grateful he had not pressed her. With Sam recovering nicely, she knew she should not put him off any longer. Hours of soul searching had only added to her confusion. Am I in love with him? When talking with Sam on the phone, she sensed her daughter's feelings for Burne had changed for the better.

Lyn dropped her purse on the chest in the living room. Turning, she found herself in Burne's arms. He cupped her face between his hands and placed a soft kiss on her lips. It started as a gentle caress, but Lyn responded freely and Burne deepened the kiss. A gasp worked its way from her throat. Lyn's senses were whirling, and her brain refused to function. Strange feelings coursed through her body, and she could feel her heart pounding in her chest. A tremor shook her entire being.

Burne tightened the embrace. One hand moved to her back, and he stroked her body from shoulder to thigh.

Her legs were weak, and she was warm all over. Her hands trapped between them, she splayed her palms against Burne's chest. His body felt hot beneath the thin fabric of his shirt. She had a sudden desire to touch his bare skin, but kept her hands between them.

Burne pulled his mouth from hers and looked into her eyes.

Their deep blue color had darkened to purple. He lifted her in his arms and carried her to the sofa. His hands trembled slightly as he touched her.

A warning bell sounded deep in Lyn's brain. What was she doing? What was she allowing Burne to do? True, he had asked her to marry him, but he had no right—*they* had no right—to...to...Her body had betrayed her, but she had to stop him while she still had the willpower. She struggled to free herself.

Lost in the pleasure, Burne was slow to notice Lyn's reaction. She tried to push him away, and his passion-drugged mind finally grasped that she wanted him to stop. "Burne," though her voice was barely audible, it managed to penetrate his dulled senses. He released her, sat up and dropped his head in his hands.

"My God, Lyn, I'm sorry!" His voice was hoarse.

Lyn knew she was just as much to blame as Burne. It was a woman's responsibility to keep things from getting out of hand. "No, don't apologize, Burne. It was just as much my fault as it was yours."

"No, sweetheart," he told her. "I should have had better control. Especially after what you went through because of one bastard who couldn't keep his pants zipped. The only excuse I have is that I want you so bad, it's eating me alive."

"Oh, Burne, I don't know what to do! I have these *feelings* when you kiss me and touch me, and I don't want you to stop." Her face was pink with embarrassment.

"I know, honey," he grinned ruefully. Standing, he ran his hand through his hair and turned to face her. "Now that Sam is recovering, we need to talk about the future. I recall asking you to marry me. You haven't given me your answer." Anxiety was written on every line of his face.

Suddenly, the answer she was seeking was there. She smiled, her blue eyes alight with love, as she answered "Yes, oh yes, Burne, I'll marry you."

As soon as the words were out of her mouth, he caught her in a fierce embrace and kissed her hard on the mouth. "I love you, Lyn," then he kissed her again, this time gently and tenderly.

She buried her face in his shoulder, and her voice was muffled when she said, "I love you, too."

He hugged her tightly, then raised her head and looked into her flushed face. "Sweetheart, when we make love the first time, I don't want you to have any doubts or feel guilty. I want to show you how wonderful it can be when two people really love each other."

CHAPTER FIFTEEN

"I'll pick up Sam after the association meeting." Lyn told her mother over the phone. "Janet and Cathy want her to spend the day with them tomorrow." She swiveled her chair to face the windows. Beyond the patio, The Manor grounds were lush and green. A regular watering schedule kept the grass and flowers thriving.

"Are you sure she's well enough, Lyn? You know how sick she was," Mrs. DeVinney's voice was filled with concern.

"Yes, I talked with the doctor this morning, and he assured me it would be all right. Besides, I know you and Dad could use some rest." Lyn glanced at the clock. She wanted to leave early.

"Now Lyn, you know your father and I love taking care our grandchildren. Especially since we don't get to do it very often."

"I really appreciate your help these past few days, Mom. The health department can be difficult if the charting isn't kept up-to-date." Lyn nodded in sympathy as she watched one of the men on the mowing crew remove his straw hat and wipe his face with a bandanna. Scorching summer heat was the price one paid to enjoy the mild winter temperatures.

"Yes, I can imagine," Mrs. DeVinney replied. "Lyn, there's something I've been wanting to ask you. I hope you won't think I'm interfering, but will you leave Texas after you're married?"

Lyn swiveled her chair around and picked up the pen lying on her desk. She had thought about the answer to that question, but she had no answer. There were so many things she and Burne needed to discuss before they could plan a wedding.

"I honestly don't know Mother. With Sam's illness, the extra hours I've been working, and Burne's problems at work, we haven't had a chance to talk about it. We're getting together Sunday and try to work out some of the details." She doodled on the pad in front of her.

"I'm glad you're not going to rush into this, dear. It's a serious step and there's Sam to consider."

"I'm well aware of that, believe me. No, Burne and I will not *rush* into it. After all, we're both mature adults and, since he's waited this long to marry, I'm sure he'll be willing to wait until we can work everything out."

"He hasn't been married before?"

"No, Mom, he hasn't." She glanced at the clock. "I need to finish a couple of things before I can leave here. The meetings are usually over by nine so I should be able to pick up Sam shortly after that. And, Mom, the family should get together soon so Burne can meet everybody."

"Yes, we need to do that. Let's talk about it tonight."

* * *

"But, son, she…"

"She what, Dad?" Burne's voice was cold. The two of them were sitting in Lawrence's living room.

"She…she doesn't seem like a very…very conscientious person. I told you how I was treated when they served those spoiled fish in the dining room."

"Dad, we talked about that. Lyn was not responsible for your *illness*. Besides, I remember the times when you were living with Annie. You didn't blame her. Why are you determined to blame Lyn?"

"Those fish were spoiled!"

Burne shook his head. It was no use trying to reason with Lawrence. The silence grew lengthy.

"Well…you haven't known her very long, and the child is…illegitimate." Lawrence tried another tactic.

"What's that got to do with anything?" Burne clenched his fists as he tried to restrain his rising temper. "I plan to adopt Sam, if she's willing."

Lawrence's eyes went wide, and he half rose from his chair. "Adopt her? Do you think that's wise? After all, you don't know anything about the child's father, what kind of family he comes from, what kind of person he is or…" his voice trailed off.

A dark flush crept up Burne's neck and he gritted his teeth to keep from lashing out at his father's callous remarks.

"I know everything I need to know. What happened is in the past and, besides, it's nobody's business." Burne was seething, and it manifested itself in his expression and the rigid set of his body.

"I…I'm sorry if I upset you, son. I just don't want to see you make a big mistake, that's all. I can't help but wonder what your mother would say if she were alive," Lawrence ended on a note of self-pity.

"You know Mother would never have condemned a person without giving them a chance. You both tried to teach us compassion and understanding. I like to think you succeeded."

A knock sounded at the door, and Burne hurried to answer, glad of the interruption. Myra and Joe were standing in the hallway.

"We wondered if you were ready to go down to dinner?" Myra asked as she stepped into the foyer.

Burne was never sure just what followed after that since his emotions were in a turmoil. Somehow Myra sensed something was amiss and, before Burne knew it, she was involved in the discussion.

"Lawrence MacKenzie, I'm ashamed of you!" Myra shook her finger at him. "Lyn is an exceptional young woman, and she will make Burne a fine wife. As for Sam, the child isn't to blame, and I know Burne will be a wonderful father."

Burne grinned at the indignant woman. Then, his expression serious, he told her, "I appreciate your support, Myra. Please don't say anything to anyone here at The Manor. Lyn and I have a lot of details to work out, and I don't want her to go through all the speculation that's bound to surface."

"I promise I won't say a word. But you do have our sincere congratulations, *doesn't he, Joe?*" Myra nudged her silent husband. He had not taken part in the discussion.

Joe offered Burne his hand. "You sure do, son. We think a lot of that little lady, and I say you're a lucky man."

* * *

Lyn and Burne were seated in the living room after a trip to Ramiro's Pizza for dinner. Sam had chosen the restaurant. After watching a video, Lyn sent her off to bed.

Burne joined Lyn on the sofa, placed his arm around her shoulders and drew her close.

"I've been wanting to do this all evening," he whispered as he kissed her. It was slow and lazy, his tongue outlining her lips as he coaxed her mouth open. She responded hesitantly at first but soon felt her pulse stirring and heat spreading through her body.

Their tongues met in a duel of love. When he thought his lungs would burst, he tore his mouth away, drawing in great gulps of air.

Stroking her cheek with his fingers, he looked into her eyes. They were heavy-lidded and slightly unfocused. His heart swelled in his chest with the knowledge that he was unlocking her frozen emotions.

"Burne." Lyn's voice was husky. "There are so many things we need to talk about, I don't know where to start."

"Let's start with a wedding date." He leaned against the back of the sofa, taking her with him and holding her close. "When are you going to marry me? Tomorrow, the next day, when?"

Laughing softly, Lyn smiled and it did crazy things to his blood pressure. "I don't think we can arrange it that quickly. You live in Indiana and I live in Texas. That could present a problem."

"I've been thinking about that. I had planned to leave San Antonio this fall, but I can stay until the project is completed. As a matter of fact, the company would be glad if I did. That will take at least another year."

"I would hate to leave Texas, but I know your work is in Indiana."

"We don't have to worry about that now. Would you like to keep this apartment or move to something larger?" he asked as he stroked her arm. Her skin felt like satin.

"I don't think we should move. At least for a while. That is, if you think you could be comfortable here." She looked up at him, her eyes dark with feeling.

"I can be comfortable anywhere as long as I'm with you," he answered as he gently eased her down on the sofa. When she started to protest pointing to Sam's door, he whispered, "It's all right. I just need to hold you in my arms and feel your body against mine."

Using every ounce of control he possessed, he pressed her slender body to his. Her arms went around him as he held her tight. He seemed to be trying to absorb her into himself. His lips nuzzled her throat and worked their way to her mouth. The kiss was barely controlled passion, hard and hot. With a deep groan he released her and sat up.

"Lady, you're either going to have to marry me right quick or shoot me and put me out of my misery!"

Her laughter was soft on his ear as she told him. "I certainly don't want to shoot you so I guess I had better set the date. I don't want a large wedding. But I would like to be married in my church, and it takes time to make the arrangements. How does six months sound?"

Burne was on his feet in an instant, pulling her into his arms. His kiss was gentle and sweet as he looked deep into her eyes and whispered, "I love you."

* * *

"We're going to put two men on stake out tonight," Sergeant Soliz told Burne the next day.

"I'm glad to hear that. We want to contain our losses as much as possible. Would it be OK if I hung around?"

"Well…I guess so. But it really isn't necessary."

Burne heard the hesitation in the detective's voice.

"Maybe not, but this is my project, and I need to know what is going on."

"OK. Our men will show up right after dark, but you won't see them. Make sure you stay in your office out of sight. We don't want to mistake you for one of the thieves."

The sky turned a pale gray as the last rays of the sun disappeared over the horizon. Burne stood on the skeleton of the fourth floor of the medical tower building. Lights were coming on all over the city and created a multicolor picture of shapes and shadows. Heights did not bother him but, then if they did he would not have the job with Williams Bohrn. It was necessary for him to personally check out details from time to time. Andy had told him he did not think the riveters were doing a good job. After a thorough inspection, Burne agreed. He would have to speak with Pete about it.

Letting his eyes roam over the construction site, Burne saw a dark blotch near one of the tool sheds. Was it a thief or one of the security guards? And where were the cops on stake out? He suddenly realized he was silhouetted against the skyline and made a perfect target for somebody bent on eliminating a witness.

Back on the ground, Burne headed toward the office. As he reached to unlock the door, he felt a faint brush of air on the back of his neck. He turned and a solid object connected with the side of his head. The multicolored lights he had seen from the tower flashed in front of him, and then vanished. Blackness descended and he felt himself falling into the void.

"He's coming around," the disembodied voice came from a long distance away.

Sharp pain roared through Burne's head. He tried to open his eyes but his eyelids were too heavy. He sensed rather than felt he was lying on the couch in the office. Struggling to sit up, a large hand pushed him back down.

"Take it easy, buddy. You took a pretty hard rap on the noggin'."

Burne thought the voice belonged to Detective Brandenburg.

"What...happened?" Burne remembered fishing in his pocket for the keys before his head exploded. Pure instinct directed his hand to the side of his head. It was sticky and he felt a ridge above his ear. He managed to hold up his hand. The smears on his fingers looked like blood.

"We're not sure but we think the perps came looking for more valuable merchandise." Detective Delgado took up the story.

"Did you catch them?" Burne's voice was raspy and his throat felt parched.

The detectives glanced at one another, then Delgado answered. "Yeah."

"Who?" Burne's vision blurred and his head ached like a thousand hammers were pounding inside.

"That can wait. The emergency guys will be here in a minute or two. We need to get you to a hospital. Any preference?" The words were hardly out of Brandenberg's mouth when the door swung open and a pair of E.M.Ts. burst inside.

Burne was loaded on a stretcher and into an ambulance before he could gather his scattered wits. Since he had not indicated which hospital, Delgado instructed the medical team to take him to University Hospital as fast as possible.

* * *

"Mr. MacKenzie, you have a concussion and a nasty head wound. You will need to stay here overnight, at least." The emergency room doctor was a young man with disheveled hair and a harried look.

"I need to let Andy know about this. He's the project engineer. His phone numbers are on a card in my wallet. And Doc, tell Andy not to let Lyn know about this. Her daughter has been very ill, and I don't want to upset her any further."

"I will take care of it, Mr. MacKenzie." The attending nurse volunteered. She was a middle-aged woman with the look of a person that has seen nearly every injury and illness known to man.

"Thanks." Burne's voice faded away.

The doctor and the nurse exchanged glances. "Mrs. Galvan, keep a close eye on Mr. MacKenzie until we can get in touch with his partner. We don't want him drifting off to sleep just yet."

"Yes, doctor. I'll tell Judy. She will cover the desk."

Mrs. Galvan brought the admission forms for Burne to sign and ask about insurance coverage. The cards were in his wallet.

Burne spent the night in the hospital. Andy picked him up the next morning and took him to his apartment. His headache was better but had not subsided completely. The doctor gave him a prescription and told him not to go back to work for a few days.

"I notified the home office," Andy told him. "Deckard was pretty upset and said he would call you this morning."

Burne grinned. "Yeah, I know how *sensitive* our GM is."

Andy chuckled. Deckard's reputation as a hardboiled construction boss was legend. "Is there anything I can get you? Anything you need?"

"No, and thanks, Andy. I appreciate all you've done. I owe you, buddy."

"You don't owe me a thing. Have you forgotten the time when Shelley was in labor and things didn't look too good for her or the baby?"

Burne shook his head. Shelley had required a blood transfusion after the baby's birth and Burne was a match. "No, but the main thing is she and the baby both came through it. And look at them today. If you hadn't married Shelley, I would have asked her myself. And Amy is a beautiful little girl."

"Yeah, I'm a lucky guy. If you do need anything, give me a call."

"Will do."

Lyn would be expecting to hear from him and he dreaded telling her about his injuries. Before he could dial her number, the phone rang. When he answered, he found himself talking with his superior in Indianapolis.

"Andy told me what happened. Are you alright?" Deckards' voice boomed out.

"Yeah, I'm OK. Just a little woozy."

"You take it easy now. Any need for me to fly down there?"

"I don't think so. That is unless you just want to take a few days off. This is an interesting place."

"I've been there, remember?" Deckard growled.

Burne recalled the original meetings when Williams Bohrn landed the contract for the towers. Several times during the negotiation process Deckard had locked horns with the city fathers. "I'm not likely to forget that."

"Well, keep me posted. And if you need anything from this end, let me know."

Taking a deep breath, he punched in Lyn's phone number.

"Dining Services, Lyn DeVinney."

Burne's heartbeat accelerated. He could picture her slender form and intense blue eyes. "Lyn, I'm sorry I haven't called before now but…but there was a little disturbance at the job site last night."

"Disturbance? What kind of disturbance?" Lyn's voice held an anxious note.

"I'm fine and I don't want you to worry." Burne filled in the details, minimizing his part in it.

"Oh, Burne, are you sure you're all right? I can leave early and come to your apartment. You probably need a nourishing meal. And how about your head wound? Does it need a new dressing? If you need errands run…"

Burne grinned. "Whoa, lady. All I need is you, but you've had enough worry with Sam and need to take a break. Andy is going to drop in later. I plan to go to the job site for awhile tomorrow and then drive up to Mt. Laurel."

"Oh, no, Burne. As much as I would love to see you, I don't think you should rush things. You need to rest for a few days." Lyn's concern colored her words.

"Don't worry sweetheart. Everything is going to be OK."

* * *

I'm glad that's over, but I'm sorry it turned out to be Carlos," Burne and Andy were discussing the situation.

The police apprehended the men responsible for the stolen goods. Carlos Romero, in cahoots with Ray Flowers, had carried out the operation. Passed over twice for an apprenticeship in the steel workers union, Carlos decided to soothe his wounded pride by fattening his wallet at the company's expense. The scheme the two men devised was simple. Flowers delivered only a portion of the material to the site, but Carlos signed for the entire order. Using an abandoned shed on his father's property to store the loot, Carlos fenced the material or sold it at the flea markets that were popular in San Antonio. Flowers received one-half of the spoils for his part in the illegal activities.

The success of their small operation led to the thieves' desire for bigger gain. More valuable tools and equipment were stored in one of the tool sheds and it became their target. Carlos and Flowers decided to take the risk. Flowers was responsible for Burne's injuries.

"Yeah, me too. It will be hard on Dan, though. He trusted Carlos."

"Well, I guess that's the way it goes," Burne shook his head as he plopped down at his desk.

"Now you can concentrate on becoming a married man and giving up your wild bachelor ways," Andy ribbed him.

Burne grinned. He wasn't going to cooperate with Andy's attempt to put him on the defensive. "You're right. It's time to settle down and let myself go. You know, get fat and all."

"Fat?" Andy growled. He had to work at keeping his weight down. "Shelley says I'm just right."

"She's the one you have to please."

"You're learning ol' buddy, you're learning."

* * *

Burne appeared at Lyn's door that evening. The white bandage above his ear contrasted sharply with the tan he had acquired since his arrival in San Antonio. She took one look at Burne and pulled him inside the apartment.

"Oh, Burne, are you sure you're alright?" Lyn was in his arms before he could close the door.

No doubt now about this woman's feelings for him. Burne grinned. *I'll have to get knocked on the head more often.*

"I'm fine. But a kiss would make me feel better."

Blue eyes met gray ones and then there was no color at all. Burne savored her soft lips and let his tongue linger at the corner of her mouth.

"I thought it was about time for that mushy stuff!" Sam's voice penetrated the silence.

Burne raised his head and saw the girl standing a few feet away. He made no move to break the embrace. "Hi, Sam."

"Hey, I want to hear all about the robbery. Did the crooks have guns, did anybody get shot…"

"Whoa, don't get carried away. I'll tell you all about it later." Turning to Lyn, he asked, "Have you talked with Dad since it happened?"

"Yes, and you need to call him right away. He knows about the robbery, but he doesn't know you were injured."

"I know I should have called him, but I didn't want to alarm him. He gets upset so easily these days. I'll drop by The Manor on my way home."

"That's a good idea. If he sees you it will be easier for him."

* * *

Before returning to his apartment, Burne drove to The Manor. The elder MacKenzie showed his usual sour disposition.

"Shelburne you should be ashamed of yourself. I am your father, and you did not see fit to notify me that you were injured."

"I know, Dad, and I'm sorry. But it happened late at night and I thought it best not to disturb you." Try as he might, Burne could not summon up any guilty feelings.

"I would rather be disturbed than not know what is happening to my son." Lawrence was not eager to accept what he knew was the best decision.

After assuring his father he was all right and relating a few of the details of the attempted robbery, Burne left The Manor. He admitted he was more tired than he realized and headed for his apartment.

* * *

"Can you leave early this afternoon?" Burne asked Lyn, his voice barely containing the excitement he was feeling.

"How early and why?"

"I have a surprise for you and Sam, and I want to show it to you as soon as possible. Can you leave, say an hour, earlier? We can grab a quick bite someplace and still have plenty of daylight to see the…" Burne mentally kicked himself. He had almost given it away.

"See what, Burne?" His excitement was contagious.

"Like I said, it's a surprise. What time shall I pick you up?"

Lyn thought for a moment. "Is four o'clock early enough?"

"That should give us enough time. I can hardly wait to see you." His voice was low and seductive.

She laughed softly. "I believe the feeling is mutual."

An undercurrent of excitement colored their mood while they dined on sandwiches and salad. Burne wouldn't give them so much as a hint about his surprise. "You have to wait until you see it," was his stock answer when Sam tried to trick him into revealing it. Lyn merely smiled, thinking about the bond that was forming between her daughter and the man who had captured her heart.

As they turned into an oak shaded street with its gracious old homes from another century, Lyn's curiosity did a reverse turn. What were they doing in this part of Mt. Laurel? She knew one or two people who lived in the area, but she rarely saw them. Before she could question him, Burne pulled up in front of a deserted house. It was one of the few that had not been kept in good condition or restored to its former glory. The roofline was broken up with a turret, dormers, gables and several chimneys. One room extended forward and projected out in front and a porch wrapped around the remainder of the front and adjoining side.

Burne cut the ignition. Sam, sitting at attention behind him, was all eyes as she questioned, "Nobody lives here so why are we stopping?"

Turning to Lyn, his gray eyes silver in their brightness and laughter in his voice, he replied, "Oh, somebody I know might live here someday."

Lyn was speechless, her expression dazed. A glimmer of understanding began to penetrate. How did Burne know... Hopping out of the vehicle, he quickly rounded it and opened the door to assist her. Sam bounded out of the Suburban and ran up the front walk. Burne held Lyn's hand as they followed Sam and climbed the steps.

Struggling to find her voice, she turned to him. "Burne, what is this all about?"

He grinned and hugged her to his side. "Let's go inside and look around." Fishing a key from his pocket, he unlocked the door. They stepped into a wide central hall running the width of the house. An elegant curving stairway led to the second floor.

Sam began exploring in earnest leaving Lyn and Burne standing in the hallway.

"Burne, if you don't tell me what's going on, I'm going to scream."

He chuckled, took her hand and led her into what obviously had been the parlor. "Since there isn't any furniture, I guess we'll have to stand," he said, looking around the empty space.

The room was blessed with an abundance of light from three tall narrow windows that formed a semi-circle facing the street, and two on the opposite wall. A wide doorway opened into another large room with a fireplace in one end. From the floor-to-ceiling bookshelves, they knew it must have been the library.

"I found out about this house by accident and checked it out. Seems the owners are anxious to sell and will let it go *as is* for a good price." He draped an arm around her shoulder, pulling her close.

Lyn could only gape. She had not thought about owning a house after she and Burne were married. At least, not in Texas.

"Come on. What do you think?"

She shook her head. "I don't know what to think. I'm completely overwhelmed."

He pulled her close and hugged her tightly. "You know, I can do most of the work myself. I'm pretty good with a hammer and saw, if I do say so myself," he told her, waving his arm in an expansive gesture.

Lyn had a lump in her throat as big as Texas, and her eyes were misty. All her secret dreams were coming true, and she could hardly take it in.

Burne was quick to notice her tears and gathered her into his arms. "I didn't know I was going to make you cry."

"I...I can't help it. How did you know I've always wanted a house like this? I never told anyone except my family."

"I know, sweetheart," he replied, placing a soft kiss on her lips.

"They told me. You do realize it's going to take a lot of work and a sizable investment to restore it?"

"I'm not afraid of hard work, and I have a little money saved. We can use it."

"Save it for those antiques you'll want to buy. Now, are you ready to see the rest of this place?"

They discovered a large dining room and kitchen plus a roomy pantry and a sunny breakfast room. The house was structurally sound, Burne had made sure of that, but years of neglect had dulled the oak woodwork and floors. The wallpaper was faded and dirty.

"Mom! Burne! Come and see this weird room," Sam called from upstairs. She had discovered the room beneath the turret roof. When told they might be living in the house, she claimed it for her own.

The spacious master bedroom was located at the back of the second story, and the large bathroom boasted a claw-footed tub and pedestal lavatory. Besides the turret room there were three more bedrooms and a smaller room next to the master bedroom.

"What do you suppose this was used for? A study, maybe," Burne asked as they surveyed the small room.

A teasing glint danced in Lyn's eyes as she answered, "It was probably a nursery."

Burne stood stock still as her remark sunk in. He turned to face her, the words frozen in his throat.

Lyn read the unspoken question in his eyes. Her lips curved in a gentle smile as she nodded. Their lips met in a kiss filled with promise.

"I didn't intend to do this until later when we were alone, but now seems like the perfect time." Burne reached a hand into his pocket and removed a small jeweler's box. He opened it and said, "I hope you like it, but it can be exchanged if you don't."

Lyn's eyes widened as the diamond reflected a shower of brilliance. It was elegant in its simplicity. A single stone set in a gold band. She gazed at the ring, then lifted her head to look at him. New tears were forming at the corner of her eyelids.

"Hey, lady, it seems like all I've done today is make you cry." He grinned and slipped the ring on her finger. It was a bit too large.

"Oh, Burne," Lyn's voice was choked as she tried to tell him how she felt. "I…I…it's perfect. I'm sorry. I love it. It's so beautiful. I'm so happy I can't help crying."

Burne pretended to breathe a sigh of relief. "I'm glad, sweetheart. I was afraid you wouldn't like it. You know, the style and all. It's plain but it seemed to be right for you. It can be resized. There is a matching wedding ring we can pick up later. Now, give me a kiss and let's find Sam."

* * *

Back at the apartment, Lyn and Burne huddled around the dining table with pads and pencils while Sam watched TV in the living room.

"If you're sure it's what you want, I'll contact Mr. and Mrs. Hummell and make an offer." Burne pushed back from the table.

Lyn's head was bent over the pad filled with figures. She looked up, her eyes shining with happiness. "Want it? Oh, Burne, it's a dream come true. But what about your job? Surely you can't commute from Texas?" Her voice betrayed her uncertainty.

"I was saving the other part of the surprise for last, but I probably should have told you about it first," he admitted. "I'll have to go to Indy in a day or two. I'll probably be there for a week or so. The company has offered me the district field manager's job. He's retiring about the time this project will be finished."

"What does that mean?" Lyn asked, confused.

"It means, my darling wife-to-be, a hefty raise in salary for starters, but the most important change will be that I won't have to stay on a job site. I will have to travel but only for short periods. I can do that from Texas as well as Indiana. With the computer hook-up, Internet, fax machines, et cetera, it doesn't make much difference where we live. I know you would go to Indiana with me, but it would be easier for Sam if we stayed in Texas. She doesn't need that kind of change in addition to all the other adjustments that are going to be necessary."

This time Lyn could not hold back the tears, and they ran silently down her cheeks. After the long years of shame, embarrassment and struggle, she was going to have a normal life with a husband and a home and, at last, Sam would have a father who loved her and wanted her.

EPILOGUE

Childish laughter broke the silence of the sunny spring afternoon. The woman watched the toddler as he played at her feet, her face reflecting an inner joy that deepened the blue of her eyes and the color in her cheeks. She smiled, her mind going back in time. How could she have been so afraid of love and commitment? The past four years had been filled with more happiness than she thought possible. There had been problems, of course, but love and patience had overcome the obstacles.

Lyn had stayed at The Manor for a year after her marriage but was now a consultant to several facilities in the area. She set her hours and fee, and it was working out quite well. Burne still traveled to various job sites but was usually away a few days at a time. Only an occasional trip to Indiana was necessary.

"Honey, I'm home."

The familiar voice startled her, but she felt her pulse flutter and her heart skipped a beat. Looking up she saw the door open, and a tall man stepped outside. His shirt was unbuttoned and his tie hung loosely around his neck. He grinned and reached for her, hugging her tightly.

"You're home early. I thought you wanted me to pick you up at the airport. How did you get home?"

"I took an earlier flight then hitched a ride. Are you complaining, Mrs. MacKenzie?" Burne asked as he kissed her waiting mouth.

Lyn shook her head as she bent to pick up the squealing little boy. "Not at all, Mr. MacKenzie," she replied as she gave him a smoldering look from under her lashes.

Burne felt his body respond, but his attention was quickly diverted by the little arms that reached out to him.

"Daddy!"

He felt as if his heart were being squeezed by giant claws as he took his son in his arms. When the child was born shortly before their second anniversary, it was then he realized the true meaning of their marriage vows. Lyn was everything he ever hoped and dreamed of, and Sam his daughter in every respect but one, and that had never mattered.

He kissed the top of his son's head and hugged the child to him. "I missed you, Davey. Have you been a good boy?" With a solemn look, the child nodded. "Yes." Then his face broke into a grin, and Lyn saw her husband as he must have looked at that age. Her eyes grew misty and a lump formed in her throat. She swallowed hard and asked, "Are you hungry? I didn't plan anything special for dinner since I thought we would eat in San Antonio."

"I don't need anything special. I already have everything I want." Burne responded, looking over his son's blond head, the stormy gray of his eyes melting into the dark blue of hers.

Their gaze held and Lyn felt desire spread through her body. Burne had unlocked passions she had never known she possessed. Her love for him had grown until she could not imagine life without him. It was as if she had not lived before him, merely existed in a vacuum filled with the necessary rudiments of every day life.

"Where's Sam?" he asked.

Lyn smiled knowingly. "She's at Cathy's. They're working on a project for their science class. She's going to stay for dinner."

He saw the invitation in her eyes and felt his blood heating up. Not willing to be ignored any longer, Davey squirmed in Burne's arms and began to fuss.

"It's time for a nap." Lyn turned toward the house.

Her denim cut-offs and oversized shirt emphasized a figure that had filled out since Davey's birth. His mind's eye conjured up a picture of Lyn's softly curved body, her ivory skin gleaming in the moonlight that flooded their bedroom. What that woman did to his libido was indecent!

With Davey sleeping soundly, Burne shut the door to their bedroom. The old Victorian house had been beautifully restored with minor alterations to accommodate twentieth century living. The small room that Lyn had identified as a nursery was ideally located to keep a close watch on their active little boy. The kitchen had undergone complete renovation supplementing the Victorian style with ultra-modern appliances.

Soft shades of blue and green, accented with rose and cream, complimented the polished oak furniture Lyn had found in her search for authentic pieces. The only concession to modern convenience was the king size bed.

Burne stripped down to his briefs in smooth quick movements. Then he was holding her close, his lips claiming her in a kiss that told of the pent up desire coursing through his body. Her passionate response sorely strained his control. Releasing her, he unbuttoned her shirt, and tossed it aside. He unsnapped her shorts and pushed them down her legs. She stepped out of them and stood before him clad in pale blue satin panties and bra. He sucked in his breath and brought her up tight against him. Her arms went around his neck, and her breasts rubbed against his bare chest. He felt her nipples peak through the slippery fabric. Sweeping her up in his arms, he deposited her in the middle of the bed and followed her down. He looked deep into her eyes, and his voice was ragged with desire as he asked, "Do you have any idea how much I love you, Mrs. MacKenzie?"

Her smile was pure seduction as she answered, "Why don't you show me, Mr. MacKenzie?"

THE END

RECIPE FOR A Happy Home

Husband
Wife
Children
Home
Generous Portions of Prayer
3 cups Love, firmly packed
package Work
package Playing Together
1 portion Patience
1 portion Understanding
1 portion Forgiveness
1 cup Kisses

Mix thoroughly, sprinkle with awareness. Bake in a moderate oven of everyday life, using as fuel all the grudges and past unpleasantness. Cool, turn out onto a platter of cheerfulness. Garnish with tears and laughter in large helpings.

Recipe Index